# Love On The Westside

Riley West

# Contents

# Introduction

I have chosen to use the Atkinson Hyperlegible typeface as well as enhance readability by using a ragged-right alignment spacing instead of indentation to delineate paragraphs. This was done with thought and purpose as a Dyslexic and Autistic person. The hope is that it makes the book a more enjoyable read. Thank you to Vellum for providing the option.

# 1

Despite her name and silver fringed hair, Lila was no manic pixie dream girl. She thought of herself as serious and driven; others called her brooding and cold. She became good at shrugging off other's opinions. At age of twenty-seven, she simply had zero fucks left to give. And it was glorious.

She chopped her hair off into a bastardized bob and bleach/dyed it to its current silvery purple perfection, left her never present anyway, sort of boyfriend, and moved to New York City. Well, came back to NYC after bouncing around the country trying to avoid her parents, who lived in the sheltered environs of Pasadena, California.

The West Coast was not her thing. Lila wasn't opposed to the sun per se, however, she much preferred the variable weather of the East Coast to the unchanging perfection of Southern California's climate. She may have also had a slight obsession with coats.

She previously escaped to New York for grad school, bewildering her mother by choosing to focus on art restoration instead of an expected medical degree—her father was a doctor, her grandfather had been one, and so on. It certainly wasn't the first time the eldest of the two Croft siblings strayed from the expected path, and even more certainly not the last.

Lila simply had no desire to stick to the status quo of her peer group or the expectations of her parents. So, when after grad school, the only job she'd been able to find in her chosen field was one back in the Golden State, it disappointed her. She was ready to be far away from her old life.

Though not being one to let her circumstances bring her down for long, Lila threw herself into her work, and gave little thought to the social machinations that were consuming the lives of her contemporaries.

One day, though, she put her paintbrush down, stepped away from the canvas, and blinked. How long had it been since she talked to another living being? Of course, there were the typical pleasantries exchanged between co-workers, grocery store clerks, etc. Phillip, her on-again off-again boyfriend, was at the time, away on business and she realized it was months since she had a proper in person conversation.

Lila wasted no time. She looked for, and found a low-level job back in New York, and was all too happy to take it. She hoped that a change of scenery would make the difference, and for a while, it did in fact, seem to work. Her first three weeks back in the city were a flurry of drinks with old friends, apartment hunting, and landing what she hoped would be a step towards her dream job; working as an art conservator at the Metropolitan Museum of Art.

She would never get rich off the job, but hell, she loved it. It was nothing to pop in her earbuds, turn up the volume, and lose herself in the warm tones and soft brushstrokes of Caravaggio or the brusque deep blacks and stark whites of Rembrandt. Her work was solitary, but she never felt alone among the canvases and paint brushes.

The solitariness of her existence outside of work, however, pricked at her. The newness of her return waned, and with it, she found her old New York friends more and more engrossed once more with their own lives. They were starting families of their own, moving out of the city. Dinner and drinks with them involved schedules and clearing it with boyfriends or spouses instead of the spontaneous late nights of the old days. Others were simply swamped at work, finishing up school, or just didn't care anymore.

So, once again, she was alone. And it was fine, Lila tried to tell herself. She'd been an outlier her entire life, never quite fitting in with any given crowd. *What does it matter now?* But as the trill of crisp autumn air made its way through the last of the dog days of summer, the loneliness creeped back in—the email she'd received from her ex, Phillip, didn't help.

He showed up a few days before, unannounced as always, looking good, a wide grin on his handsome face, and she went along with it. Because why not? They'd known each other since middle school, and had been friends. Dated periodically through high school. They remained friends and got together when it was convenient.

Neither talked as if theirs was a great love, but Lila always hoped for more, if for no other reason than being with Phillip was easy. He was a known quantity, and it was a comfort to think that somewhere, someone thought enough of her to keep coming back. Still, when after their last weekend together, Lila received what amounted to a Dear John email, she couldn't help but feel jilted.

"Unfair of me to expect you to wait when I don't know when I will be back... I won't trouble you again," Phillip wrote.

*Self-important asshole*, Lila thought, If you don't want to 'trouble me', stop showing up on my doorstep looking for a place to land.

She hated to admit to herself that Phillip's email got under her skin, but dammit, it did. So much so, in fact, that when her mother announced she was coming in town for a few days and invited Lila to what she was sure would prove to be another boring charity dinner, Lila actually jumped at the chance to get out and about.

# 2

Lila was wearing her favorite coat, a worn-in black moto jacket over an expensive black cocktail dress and four-inch heels, which made her of average height. A sore subject for her, especially in a family where she stood nearly six inches shorter than anyone else, including her mother. The statuesque former model bought the dress her daughter was wearing; Lila refused to take money from her mother, but clothes were a different matter.

The woman had good taste and the black cocktail dress fit Lila like a glove. She chanced a look in the mirrored walls of the elevator and blew out a breath; she looked good, though she fully expected her mother to make some remark about the appropriateness of her attire; Janet wouldn't approve of the jacket/dress combo, she was sure. There was a ding, and the doors opened into the penthouse.

"Well," she whispered, "here we go." Lila hadn't seen her mother in months, not since moving back to New York. Six glorious months, to be precise, in which she used the legitimate excuse of work to avoid going home. She was sure as hell was not looking forward to the small talk, questions about when she was going to get married and settle down or why on earth she took an entry position in art conservation at the Met instead of returning to Pasadena. *Dodging you!* Lila answered her mother's imaginary question.

There was a moment of shocked alarm as Lila entered the Penthouse, her heels clicking against black wood floors; it was certainly not the stuffy society home she was used to. Despite following the doorman's directions, for a moment, she was afraid she was in the wrong place.

Instead of the expected porcelains and oriental rugs, the large entryway was stark white, lit with a soft glow of neon purple, a large graffiti style mural ran the length of one wall, and low-slung modern furniture dotted the landscape. A low thrum of bass was just audible beneath the din of conversation. Who was it her mother said was throwing this party? Definitely no one from her mother's usual circle; that was clear.

The crowd differed from the society snooze fest she was used to as well. As Lila meandered, snatching a glass of champagne from a server, she saw a few geezers in their tuxes, women that were way too thin with bad plastic surgery, *typical*, but there were also younger, well dressed, interesting looking people heavily scattered throughout. In fact, she was pretty sure the guy with his tongue down the throat of a ridiculously beautiful woman, just starred in a film that was about to make a billion dollars at the box office.

Annnnnnd, there was her mother, waving at her. *Ugh.* Lila downed the champagne and reached for another before making her way to the throng of blonde, tanned ladies. At least Imogen was there, the only non-blonde of the group. Her mother's boarding school roommate was about the only one of her mother's friends that didn't look at her like she had three heads.

"Hello love," Imogen's upper class English accent cut through the room, and it was the attractive brunette that opened her arms in invitation rather than Lila's mother. "Loving the jacket," the older woman said as she fondly embraced her, "and the hair. Suits you."

Lila's mother, Janet, was a bit taken aback by her daughter's appearance. Lila noticed her mother's slightly flared nostrils and imagined what she was thinking; *purple hair* (it was the lightest of light lavenders). *What statement is she trying to make now?*

Janet never separated herself from her daughter and held the mistaken belief that every single thing Lila did was a response to her. Several of Lila's therapists over the years classified her mother as narcissistic, and Lila didn't disagree. The hair color, like most of what she did, had nothing to do with her mother. She just liked the damn color.

"It's certainly different," Janet interjected as she gave Lila a brief hug.

Lila responded with a tight-lipped smile and a peck on the cheek, their customary public greeting; in private, a simple hello and wave from the other side of the room was sufficient.

Twenty minutes later, and the small talk went from annoying, "You're back in the city, I hear?" To unbearably boring and awkward, "When are you going to find someone to settle down with?"

Lila was staring intently at a ding in the floors, intent on hiding the redness of her cheeks, when the conversation ceased. "Ah!" Imogen said as she pulled at someone behind Lila. "Lila, you have to meet my little sister and the host of this gathering."

A goddess appeared; Lila couldn't breathe. The woman was all coppery curls and green eyes, and, *Oh god, that smile*. And how in the hell, Lila wondered, did her skin look like it was suffused with the last amber rays of the summer sun itself.

She said something, the heavenly creature, apparently named Kate, said something, and then, she was gone and Lila wasn't sure if it had been real, except for the heat still throbbing in her cheeks and her stomach turning cartwheels as the subtle scent of orange blossom and rose lingered.

Lila had managed to speak to the woman, she was at least sure of that. Her fingers raked across her palm, the one Kate held so briefly, she hoped her hand wasn't as hot and sweaty as it felt to her as she remembered her brief embrace of greeting with the other woman.

Imogen leaned in, placed an arm around Lila's shoulders, "Outside, you look like you're about to pass out," she steered Lila away from the throng that included her mother and onto the large balcony, "my sister can have that effect," she whispered into Lila's ear.

# 3

## Two Hours Earlier...

Imogen looked around her sister's home, complimenting the catering and event staff as she went, trying to tick off a long mental list of everything that needed to be done for this party to come off, silently cursing her sister for abandoning her hosting duties. Six months ago, it seemed a grand idea to host the charity event at her famous sister's Upper West Side penthouse.

Kate's divorce was final. There was a new show on the horizon, and Imogen thought the party would give her sister something beyond herself to focus on. But with everything that happened, Kate practically went into hiding, and currently hadn't left her studio in days. Imogen hit the last number on her cell and tried her sister's assistant again; she heard the answering ring as the elevator door opened.

"I've got her! I've got her!" came an exasperated English accent as Jenna, Kate's assistant, and the artist herself were revealed.

Imogen let out a sigh of relief, followed by a flash of irritation as she took in her sister's state. Her eyes were red-rimmed, her face puffy, lips swollen. Clearly, she'd been crying. Her clothes, hands and even bits of her hair were covered in paint and her trademark lion's mane of curls were in a top-knot that looked, as did the rest of her, like it hadn't been washed in days.

"Jesus Kate," Imogen groaned, "people are going to be here in two hours!"

"Yes, I'm aware. Jenna was very clear as she was dragging me out of my studio where I was actually getting work done for the first time in months!"

"No, you weren't," Jenna countered, "you were stuffing your face with kettlecorn and watching Downton Abbey for the thousandth time!"

"I can't!" Imogen threw up her hands. "I can't deal with the petulant, moody artist bullshit right now, Kate! You agreed to help host this party." She turned to her sister's assistant, "Jenna, help me, please!"

The tiny brunette smiled, cocked her head, and instead of giving her employer's sister what for, said, "I'm officially off the clock, I need a drink," before turning and making her way towards the bar, giving the sisters their privacy.

Kate slung her bag onto the kitchen island, barely missing a plate of hor d'oeuvres. "I told you this was a bad idea," she said.

"No, you didn't!" Imogen rebutted in the needling tone of the elder sister she was.

Kate shrugged, "Well, I meant to," her tone had changed and Imogen checked herself as she heard the hitch in her sister's voice, "and you should have known it would be. People are whispering about it everywhere I go; I don't need that in my home."

"It's been six months, Kat, its died down." She was lying, of course, but it would do no good to agree with her, Imogen knew. Instead, Imogen's lips pursed in understanding; to go through a divorce was, as she knew from personal experience, hard enough, but to do so in the very public way her sister had must have been humiliating. She wrapped Kate in a rare, warm hug. "Stop letting what that bastard did or does fuck with your life. Time to get back to the Kate we all know."

"Can't I just be new schleppy Kate, that buries herself in her work?" she grumbled.

"If it was work you were doing, that would be one thing, but we both know, as poor Jenna has just confirmed, that isn't the case."

Imogen took a breath. She knew her sister better than anyone, and the state she was in was worrying her. Her sister's divorce had been drawn out over an excruciating two-years and for the six months since its finalization, Kate holed up in her studio, isolating herself from everyone save her closest friends, which, Imogen gave her, was understandable. But, the divorce was over, Wes very much moved on and Kate simply couldn't be allowed to go down the rabbit hole of self-imposed exile she seemed determined to.

"Go take a shower, fluff the hair, and get an ice pack on your face; you're still an ugly crier." Kate glared, and again Imogen softened, "And try to relax. Jenna and I have everything under control. Right, Jenna?" she said over her shoulder. Jenna turned from the bar and gave an unenthused smile as she lifted a cocktail in salute. "See," Imogen said brightly, ignoring her sister's assistant. "Tonight is a party, it's supposed to be fun." She released Kate from the hug and nudged her with an elbow, "You may even find something, or someone, to distract yourself from all this other bullshit."

Imogen winked and Kate shook her head, but couldn't help giving what she meant as a hopeful smile. Im wasn't wrong, she needed to move on and maybe she could be comfortable enough in her own home to allow herself to be just that, herself again.

**Present**

And holy hell, was this Lila ever something distracting, Kate thought as she excused herself from their introduction and darted into her bathroom. Her head was spinning. She hadn't thought she'd drank that much. *Never get sloppy at one's own party*, was a mantra. But here she was, bracing herself against the cool cement walls of her bathroom, attempting to slow her breathing. *What in the bloody hell was that?* she thought, trying to clear her head and taking a larger than normal drink from her wineglass.

"Lila," she repeated breathlessly into the empty space. Had she made a complete idiot of herself, she wondered? Her eyes locked with the younger woman's and she'd gone on auto-pilot. Lila made some remark about Kate's name versus her sister's and she'd said something asinine and flirty? Had she really flirted with the gorgeous silver-haired beauty?

"Just Kate," she'd said in response to Lila's comment. "I guess they knew my personality was enough to handle," she'd winked at Lila, and Kate's heart stopped as she felt her cheeks flame to life and her temperature go up about ten degrees. Maybe she was having a hot flash. *Is it too early for early menopause?* Kate wondered half seriously.

*Oh, my god!* she face-palmed, remembering their interaction. Did she actually wink at Lila? Kate took another swig of wine and thought, *No one noticed, I'm sure. Besides, everyone knows I'm the most terrible flirt and none of it ever means a thing.* But that had been before; before when she was very married and very adoring and not adrift in a possible mid-life crisis. This didn't feel like it meant nothing; it felt important, like she needed to run back out there and at the very least, talk to Lila, not let this creature that sparked something in her go.

How long had it been since she'd felt this way? Kate tried to think back, and realized that since she'd been married, she hadn't allowed herself the possibility of attraction to anyone else, nor really had she felt the need. She foolishly thought her marriage was the rare kind where two people were together with no need of another living soul. She found out the hard way that she was very wrong. *Steady, old girl,* she thought as she fluffed her hair and smoothed her dress.

She looked good, damn good, and she knew it. The black silk of her dress brushed over her curves, pulled tight against her lush breasts as she raised her arms, stretched. *Time to see if I've still got it.*

# 4

Imogen smiled at Lila as they stood staring out onto the river. "My sister is the world's biggest flirt, don't pay her any mind."

Lila dropped her head onto her forearms as she gazed across the distance at nothing, letting the cool air soothe her burning cheeks. "Do you think my mother noticed?" She was embarrassed, terrified that she'd made a fool of herself, but most of all, the need to see Kate gripped her once more.

"I love your mother like a sister, a very boring, extremely self-absorbed sister," she scoffed. "I only noticed because Kate's had that effect on everyone since she was a teenager. Everyone, men, women, didn't matter, they wanted her, which always irked me a bit; technically, I'm the better looking sister, well, once upon a time I was. She is fifteen years younger than me..." Lila did some quick math, knowing that Imogen and her mother were the same age so that put Kate at forty-two.

"Too bad she has such rubbish taste," Imogen continued, "Lila, darling, I tell you right now," Imogen said emphatically, taking a long draught from her wine glass, "nothing would make me happier than seeing her with someone like you. Her ex is a real bastard, and she needs someone to just be kind to her. Things have never been easy for her, despite appearances."

Lila's interest was further piqued. A gorgeous woman with a mysterious, tragic past, how could she not be intrigued? But, she didn't know what to say. She was certainly open to dating women; definitely was attracted to them. In fact, Lila had the inkling she was far more interested in women than men. Even tried to tell her mother she liked both men and women to broach the subject. Janet said something like, "Oh, of course you don't," and brushed it off, leaving Lila standing alone in the kitchen wondering how her mother could be so oblivious. But this situation was a lot.

First, she hadn't even known, or really ever registered, that Imogen had a sister, and she'd known the woman her entire life. So where in the hell was Kate her whole life? Second, she did not know why a *woman*, and her brain stressed that word, would ever see anything in a *girl*, again, her brain stressed the word, like her. Because, despite being twenty-seven, despite living on her own since she was seventeen, despite having a proper job and a career path, finally, she didn't feel like an adult yet, and Kate seemed so clearly out of her league. First things first, though.

"Um, is she even into women?" Lila asked, allowing a tendril of hopefulness unfurling within her.

Imogen shot her a shocked look, "Oh, I mean, I didn't actually mean you, obviously," she laughed, and Lila's heart sank. Imogen noted the look of disappointment Lila was trying to take off her face, and placed a hand on her arm, "My sister is lovely in every way, but," Lila could tell Imogen was searching for the right thing to say, "she's been through a lot," still trying to figure out exactly where to draw the line, "You two are just in different places in your lives; she's too old for you, for one, and complicated, and damaged. Also, that ex-husband of hers, believe you me, you want nothing to do with him. He'd ruin you just for the fun of it. You need someone as shiny and new and bright as yourself."

Lila made some non-committal sound, "I don't think anyone has ever described me as 'shiny and bright', Im." Not to mention the fact that to her, Kate looked like the shiniest and brightest creature she'd ever laid eyes on.

Imogen placed an arm around her narrow shoulders. "I'm just glad I haven't been wrong about you all these years! I knew you were far more interesting than your mother!

"Certainly are!" came Kate's smokey voice behind them. Lila turned and saw the redhead holding out a glass of wine, which she happily took. "Now, from what I remember my sister saying, you're in art restoration."

Lila blinked, but was grateful for the conversation starter, though shocked that Imogen would have previously mentioned her to her sister or that Kate would remember. "Yeah, I am. I'm at the Met."

"Fantastic!" Kate hooked an arm through Lila's and began steering her away from her sister, whose eyes had grown round as saucers. "I want to hear all about it!"

Kate and Lila wound through the crowd, Kate muttering apologies as they moved through the throng. "Something I have to handle," the excuse she was giving to the other guests, trying to grab her attention. She didn't care. She was sure there'd be talk, but when one reached her level, when was there not? Suddenly, all her earlier fears didn't matter. *Let them gossip.* It was a party, and she meant to have fun.

A half dozen cheek kisses with partygoers and abbreviated conversations later, and the two women entered a study; the only traditional looking space in the apartment, from what Lila saw. It was a room from another time; a time of smoking jackets and cigars, and Lila wondered if this had been the so-called 'bastard of an ex's' study, as that old world masculine feel was heavy here.

Kate saw the look of confusion on Lila's face as they entered the wood paneled room. "I don't care what anyone says. A study should have wood paneling and a fireplace." She smiled and opened a sliding glass door onto a secluded balcony, complete with an outdoor fire. Kate flipped a switch and the sparkling glass shards erupted in flame.

Lila followed her hostess onto the balcony. "This is amazing," she said. The sun had finally set and the lights of the Empire State Building, amongst countless others, filled her view.

"It is, isn't it?" Kate leaned against the doorframe, watching Lila admiring the city she loved; wondering if she had ever seen it like this from such a vantage. Few did, and Kate never lost sight of just how fortunate she was to be one of them. She worked a lifetime for this view and when she and her husband, Wes, split up, the apartment was the one non-negotiable item on the table.

Kate took a deep breath, and another drink of her wine, feeling the dark liquid thrum in her veins; there was no denying what she was feeling, what she wanted. But someone like her, someone in her position, she couldn't be the one to make the first move, could she? Or had she already? Her sister, Imogen, looked astonished when she'd pulled Lila away from their conversation, but she didn't think it was any of her business frankly. She took another drink of wine to steady herself, to drop the barrier her fear and insecurity had erected. *Really, it was no one's business, dammit.*

Lila stirred as she felt Kate's warmth beside her. "The air's different up here," she said, turning to stare up into Kate's sparkling green eyes. Lila swallowed hard, feeling her heart nearly beating out of her chest as their eyes met; her hand, chancing the lightest touch against Kate's as they rested on the cold metal railing. Heat pooled in her core and she felt as if every nerve ending was sparking with desire for the woman beside her.

She thought she could feel that same need emanating from Kate as well, but she couldn't be sure. She wanted to kiss her, wanted to wrap her arms around Kate and completely lose herself in the heat of that embrace. But what if she was wrong? What if this was just the most incorrect read of a situation she'd ever made in her life? If it was, and Kate wasn't interested, if anyone found out, she cringed inwardly at the imagined embarrassment. But, as she struggled with herself,

Kate's lips parted in a faint smile, her eyes tilting up in what seemed to be a pleased acknowledgement of their touch, and Lila's heart lifted in excitement and hope.

"If it's too cold, we could go back inside," Kate offered, almost hoping Lila would say yes. The insecurities that had been absent previously came surging back in. After all, what was she doing out here with a much younger woman; a woman, period? She wasn't in boarding school anymore, for god's sake; the time for experimentation came and went a very long time ago, hadn't it?

Lila knew it was now or never, and she shook her head, her heart pounding in her chest as she took Kate's hand in hers, "I don't want to go anywhere," her voice hoarse with desire, her hip lightly pressing into Kate's.

Kate took a breath, swallowed, her hand skimming Lila's back, her insides twisting with excitement.

"Kate?" a disembodied woman's voice sounded from inside.

Kate's eyes squeezed shut at the disruption. "Bloody hell," she murmured. "Just a minute Jenna!" she shouted through the open door. Kate took Lila's hand back in hers, holding it gently but firmly, "The party should break up soon; if it doesn't, I'll make it. Let me go say my goodbyes. And then please, promise me you'll be here when I get back."

"I should say goodbye to my mom," Lila said, setting her wine-glass down and turning towards the apartment.

"No," Kate stopped her, pulling on the hand she still held; the fear of being found out suddenly rushing back in. "I'll tell her you've already gone. If that's alright?"

Lila gave Kate's hand a squeeze and smiled in what she hoped was a reassuring manner, "Then, I'll be here, and it will just be the two of us." Kate was right, Lila thought, best to let their tryst go unobserved, for now.

Kate felt the knot in her stomach unwind. The unspoken understanding of their mutual attraction affirmed. A smile lodged in the corner of her full lips, "Good, because I don't want you going anywhere either." She turned to go back inside but stopped, "I guess I should say though, make yourself at home," and with that, Kate left Lila on her own.

Lila's mouth split into a wide grin as her hand shot up to cover it. *Holy shit!* She thought, taking a large drink of her wine. Never would she have believed that something like this could happen to her. She'd never felt such an instantaneous attraction to anyone before; she wondered if it was the same for Kate? *I'm going to do this!* she told herself. Lila was not about to pass up the opportunity to be with a woman like her hostess.

She wasn't new to flings, having her share like most anyone her age, but while this certainly had the telltale signs of shaping up to be just that, Lila hoped maybe it could be more. She was the hopeless romantic type, and Kate looked like some majestic queen from a fairytale ruling above her subjects from her lofty tower.

Lila took another look at the lit city around her; the breathtaking beauty of it trying to root her to her spot, but as the night set in fully, the temperature dropped. Even with her leather jacket on, Lila was feeling the cold and as she waited for Kate, she stepped back inside the study they'd passed through. The little paneled room was cozy against the chill as Lila entered; a fire going, the smell of leather enveloping her.

"Make yourself at home," Kate had said, not that Lila took her at her word. People never really meant that, but she was free to snoop a bit.

Lila always thought people's books said a lot about them, and she was interested to see just what was on Kate's shelves. As Lila scoped out the worn and various titles housed in the floor to ceiling cases, she saw Kate didn't have a library for show; these weren't antique books by the yard or color coordinated to match the decor. There were battered copies of breezy beach reads, equally battered copies of the wordy tomes of ancient philosophers and poets, biographies on Eleanor of Aquitaine, Hatsepshut, even a few works on several of Lila's favorite artists; Old Masters. It impressed her. It would seem Kate was as avid and varied a reader as she.

"Find anything scandalous?" Lila turned to find Kate leaning against the doorframe; the tall, elegant figure she cut completely at odds with the mischievous glint in her eyes and broad smile. Lila wondered how long she'd been there, watching her.

"It's an interesting assortment."

Kate nodded towards a shelf she'd missed, "Finest collection you'll ever see on courtesans." Lila's mouth gaped as Kate shrugged, "But, mostly just things I like. I guess I don't have any one particular taste." She moved into the room, the black silk of her dress outlining the shape of her thighs as she moved closer, a smile playing on her lips. "Do you like whisky?"

Lila blinked. She did in fact love whisky, and had noted the rare vintage sitting on the 1960s style bar cart in the corner. "Um, I do. Are you trying to get me drunk?" Lila teased and immediately was struck by her overly familiar tone. She wasn't usually one to warm so quickly.

A worried look flashed over Kate's features, "No."

Lila chuckled at the look, though felt a pang of guilt for causing her host even the slightest worry. "I'm teasing you, sorry."

"Ah." Kate smiled, obviously relieved, her body visibly relaxing. "Whisky then? None of my friends like it and I haven't had the heart to drink it alone."

Kate wasn't lying about her friends not liking the stuff, but it wasn't just that she wanted to share it with someone, but at the moment, she needed it to steady her nerves. She hadn't been with anyone aside from her husband in twenty years, and her ex had done such a thorough job of destroying her self-confidence, Kate couldn't believe anyone would even want to be with her. She realized in the moment, she still needed to be wanted, and there was Lila, looking at her like, hazel eyes drinking in every move she made, dark with desire.

"That's a pretty serious bottle," Lila commented, nodding towards the ornate bottle.

"On the rocks or neat?" Kate asked.

"Neat, please." Lila's pulse quickened as Kate brushed past her; Kate's hand gliding over her leather clad shoulder as she passed. Lila downed the rest of her wine, trying to steady herself.

"My grandmother was Scottish." Kate's back was to her as she poured the drinks, giving Lila a moment to compose herself; it wasn't working. "She taught me everything I know about the stuff…"

Kate continued speaking, but Lila didn't hear a word. The figure before her was mesmerizing. Lila's eyes travelled over her as Kate poured two glasses of the smoky nectar; her mouth was dry, and she heard the thrumming of her own heart in anticipation and desire.

Kate's bare feet peaked out from beneath the black silk dress, she'd discarded her heels somewhere; still, she was tall. The word 'statuesque' sprang to mind and Lila found she wanted nothing more than to put her hands on that nipped waist and know the feel of her lips pressed to that golden skin.

"There we are," Kate turned from the cart and handed Lila a glass. "To us," she said, grinning before taking a swallow of the smooth, fiery liquid.

"To us," Lila stammered back and did likewise.

Kate moved to the leather sofa, rucking the hem of her dress up around her knees as she drew her legs up before her. Lila almost laughed. Here was this beautiful, elegantly clad woman, in a penthouse in New York, barefoot, drinking whisky, enticing her with those glittering green eyes; nothing that had happened that evening seemed real, and the woman before her, the most unreal part of it all. Normally, Lila would have slowly sipped at such a fine glass of whisky, but she downed the remaining drink in one go, relishing the smoky burn, and sank down beside her host.

Lila's hand swept up the smooth length of Kate's calf, her thumb brushing over a knee. She waited, half expecting Kate to tell her to stop, but there were those green eyes meeting hers with just as much wanting as her own.

Lila couldn't believe this was happening. Her shaking hand continued up Kate's leg, her thigh; her body following as Kate said, "Come here," in a breathy whisper, her open arms beckoning Lila onward. She reached for Kate, dipping her head for a kiss, their mouths crashing together as Lila felt Kate's hands find purchase under her bottom. She heard the rumble of Kate's groan and pulled away. She wanted to make perfectly sure this was what Kate wanted before they went any further.

Kate's eyes were round as she met them with her own. "You're not stopping, are you?" she sounded slightly panicked.

"Do you want me to?"

"God, no!" Kate cradled the back of Lila's head and pulled her back down into another kiss. Their tongues surged against each other as Lila struggled with and found the tiny zipper of Kate's dress, her hand grazing over a full breast as it did.

"How does this come off?" Lila asked, hand shaking.

"Over the head!" Kate managed, wriggling out from beneath Lila, pulling at the delicate material, not caring what happened to the expensive garment. All she cared about now was getting the damn thing off and getting her hands and mouth back on Lila.

Lila scooted back onto the sofa, propping herself up on her elbows, watching Kate as the black silk of her dress slipped up her body, over her shoulders, revealing the golden skin beneath inch by inch. The dress itself landed unceremoniously in a pile across the room; forgotten. The sight of Kate as she shook her hair back out, clad only in a plunging black lace bra and matching underwear, nearly undid Lila.

"How are you real?" Lila breathed and saw a smile ghost over Kate's lips.

"Maybe none of us are." The whisky had done its job well, and both women had gained the liquid courage they needed to continue. "That doesn't mean I'm not going to enjoy this," Kate said, covering Lila's body with her own.

Lila's hands moved up Kate's bare back as Kate's mouth worked its way up Lila's throat. Lila managed without incident to unhook Kate's bra and toss it towards the discarded dress in the corner. The move elicited a groan of pleasure from Kate, who's now freed breasts, found themselves in Lila's eager hands. Anyone who knew Lila knew she was an equal opportunity admirer of both men and women, but until now, she'd only ever been with men.

She'd wanted this though, more than she could even admit to herself. And, here she was, thumbs brushing over the exquisite nipples of this amazing woman. Kate's breasts were full, heavy in her palms, the dark peach nipples peaked. No longer capable of going slow, a needy sound rumbled low in Lila's throat and she tipped Kate back onto the sofa, fingers grasping and tightening in those red curls, her lips and teeth and tongue moving to taste and pleasure the woman writhing beneath her.

# 5

They were in the city; there were no birds, or lawn mowers, or neighbors raking leaves to wake them from their stupor; instead, it was the inevitable harsh light of day that stirred the women. The icy white light came in cold and bright off the river through the floor to ceiling windows and woke Lila with a start.

Lila's head shot up as she tried to clear her mind through the fog of alcohol and the stabbing pain in her skull. There was something soft and warm beneath her; she scrunched her eyes shut and tried to get her bearings as she wiped drool from her mouth.

"Oh. My. God!" The words were out before she could, too late, clamp a hand over her mouth. She was sprawled naked over an equally nude but much more artfully posed Kate, on the leather sofa in the middle of her very open living room. The woman looked like a goddess from a pre-raphaelite painting beneath her; the smattering of lines around eyes and mouth doing nothing to diminish her beauty, while Lila knew she must look as bad as she felt.

Lila took in the golden skin and lush breasts of her "lover"? It really happened, not that she really remembered it, and now Lila did not know what to do. What she wanted was to lie back down, fitting herself against Kate. Wanted to nuzzle up under her chin and drift off into sleep. Wanted to wake to Kate's kisses and caresses and that throaty chuckle that made her wet and never leave. There were butterflies in her stomach at the thought of being with the goddess beneath her.

"Oh, my god!" Kate's voice croaked into the new morning. Lila realized she'd been daydreaming as the body beneath her bucked and her eyes met the startled eyes of the woman she'd fucked, no, *worshipped,* the night before.

Kate struggled to untangle her body from Lila's; pulling at the thick blanket they'd both been wrapped in, trying to stand and haul the blanket with her.

"This," Kate started, "this, I, just, no!" she sputtered as understanding crashed over the beautiful daydream Lila had been having of a life with this woman. "You should leave," Kate finally managed a complete sentence. Clearly, she was flustered.

Lila's cheeks were flaming, and tears pricked at her eyes, "But, Kate! Last night!" She didn't care that she was standing naked in the middle of a living room, Kate needed to know what she felt. The connection was real, wasn't it?

Kate didn't make eye-contact. She looked everywhere but at Lila's nude form. "Please leave," she said, this time there was sadness in her tone.

Lila reached for her, But Kate stiffened, pulled the blanket tighter around herself. Lila's shoulders slumped as she searched for and found her clothes in a pile under the coffee table. She hastily dressed and said, "I'm sorry," before making her way downstairs to a cab. *Fucking walk of shame, Jesus,* she thought as she rolled up to her corner. No way she was taking the subway in her current state. *Fuck me.*

Lila's slight OCD and social anxiety kicked in by the time she made it to a cab. Now, twenty minutes later, she had re-lived their catastrophic morning a hundred times over, feeling like a bigger idiot with each go. What the hell was she thinking? *That some super wealthy socialite was just going to be like, sure, totally down for this lesbian relationship with this random girl that popped into her party. Yeah, totally feasible.* Lila dropped her head into her hands for the thousandth time.

"Uggghh," she groaned and kicked in frustrated anger and desire at the wall of her shower. If not for the events of the morning, well, at least since Kate woke up, the whole thing had been like a fantasy. And there had been Kate, a woman in her prime, gorgeous, fascinating, sexy as hell, and for one night, she'd been everything Lila could have hoped for. But now, the dream was over.

She heard her phone buzz and crawled out of the shower. Maybe it was a text from Kate? *I'm totally obsessed, dear lord!* It wasn't Kate, but Liz, Lila's best friend from back home that thankfully also lived in the city. *Shit!* They were supposed to have breakfast. She wrapped a towel around her and called Liz, who picked up immediately.

"I swear if you are still asleep," Liz said, half joking, half clearly very pissed. "I'm in K-Town at 9:30 on a Saturday, freezing my ass off. Where are you? I was promised spicy tofu soup!"

"It's the first week of September, you're not freezing anything off," Lila grumbled.

"Where are you?" Liz repeated. "It's too early and I'm too hungover for sarcasm."

"On my way, I promise! Some crazy shit went down last night. I'm just moving a little slow."

# 6

"You had sex with a cougar in her penthouse and woke up drooling on her?" Liz's spoonful of soup hung in the air, forgotten as Lila dropped her story of the night before and the disastrous morning.

Lila showed up for breakfast, definitely looking like what the cat drug in, but at least she was there. "Shh!" Lila tried to calm her friend down. The two were sitting in a corner booth of their favorite twenty-four-hour Korean BBQ place, which had an almost disturbing number of equally hungover looking Manhattanites downing the delicious spicy fare.

"I wasn't drooling on her! I mean, I'm sure that wasn't what happened; why she kicked me out, I mean. And since when does forty-two count as cougar status?" Lila looked down, still disheartened by the whole thing, but grateful for the soup that was making whisky scented sweat sheen on her forehead. Something so good had gone so wrong in so short a time.

"What happened was, Mrs. Robinson woke up and realized she banged some girl who's mom she's friends with, whoops. And, thirty-five."

"Thirty-five? What?"

"Anne Bancroft was thirty-five when she played Mrs. Robinson, the archetypal definition of a cougar."

Lila glared across the table at the useless factoid from Liz. "I don't even know if we really even had sex," Lila confessed. The night was a foggy mess, worsened by the post-drinking anxiety she was feeling.

Liz looked confused. "How's that? You woke up, on top of her, naked."

"The last thing I remember is," she hesitated, looked around to make sure no one was in earshot, embarrassed, "the last thing I remember is going down on her." Lila watched her friend as her eyes widened.

"That's sex Lila," Liz deadpanned.

"It's terrible, right?" Lila cringed.

"Not if you did it right," Liz winked. "It's a mess if your mom finds out though. How do they know each other again? She sounds way too cool to be friends with her."

"Kate's older sister was my mom's college roommate and they're all involved in some charity that does something for kids that need glasses for their foster cats, or something." Lila finally cracked a smile. "You know my mom's always got something new to give money to."

Liz rolled her eyes. "Right?" Lila's mom was always ready to help others, so long as they weren't members of her own family.

————

"Jesus," Kate was pacing, wishing like hell she had a cigarette, not that it was even legal to smoke in her own goddamn home and not that she'd smoked one since college, but at the moment, it was all she wanted. The phone on the other end continued to ring. "Fuck! Fuck! Fuck!" she swore into the device before a tired sounding woman answered.

"Hey!" the woman on the other end of the line answered. Kate wondered how her friend could sound both exhausted and chipper. "What are you doing up so early? Didn't you have a party last night? Are you calling to tell me about some amazing sex you had with some young, gorgeous thing?" Jules asked. She had three kids under four. Vicarious was her middle name. "I'm in the middle of watching the same movie for the thousandth time. So please, tell me something juicy!"

"Come over!" Kate exclaimed.

Jules' tone switched to worried, but amused. "Is there a body?"

————

"I fucked a twenty-seven-year-old!"

"Nice! You are calling to tell me about sex! I'm failing to see the problem."

"Ohmygodyoubitch," her voice was strained, "Just get over here!" Kate hung up without waiting for an answer. The phone buzzed in her hand; her sister was calling. Kate rolled her eyes, but picked up. It wasn't like Imogen to call so early and she wondered just what her sister was calling about. *Please, don't let it be about Lila!*

"I just got the strangest call," her sister said before Kate could even mutter a greeting.

Kate made a non-committal sound. "Hmm?" She didn't want to give anything away.

"It was Wes," Imogen started, and Kate relaxed. "He was calling to see how your party went; wanted to see if you had a good time."

That was strange for sure, but not worrying. Still, it made no sense for him to be calling her sister, of all people. No one, to her knowledge, in her close circle had spoken to her ex outside of a judicial setting for almost three years. What was Wes doing checking up on her?

"I can't believe you actually picked up," Kate said. Her sister was one of her most vocal advocates in the complete debacle, for which Kate would never cease to be grateful.

"Well, it was so early I didn't look to see who it was. I was still foggy you know," Kate definitely knew, her head was pounding. "Anyway," Imogen went on, "I told him it was no concern of his but that you were doing very well and that was that."

"Weird."

"Very," Imogen agreed. "You don't think it has anything to do with those rumblings about him?"

Kate rubbed at her eyes, thinking how nice it would be for coffee laced with Bailey's to magically appear in her hand. "Rumblings?"

She could see Imogen shake her head in frustration at her through the phone; she'd been living in something of a bubble for months. "I've heard there may be some legal troubles coming down on him, money issues. Your lawyers haven't spoken to you?"

Kate shut her eyes, took a deep breath. Whatever problems Wes had now, were no longer hers. "Im, I'm sorry he called you, but I don't care what he's up to at this point." And, she realized with a bit of joy, she actually meant it. Maybe last night hadn't been a terrible mistake after all, if it meant she wasn't brooding about her ex.

"Well, I'm glad, but probably talk to your lawyers. Just make sure nothing that asshole has done can blow back on you."

Kate was so not in the mood to talk about Wes, or money, and definitely not lawyers. "I'll give them a heads up Monday, but if you know about it, I have a feeling they probably do as well."

"Let's hope so for what you pay them!"

"Precisely." *Ok,* she thought, *please let me go crawl into a dark hole now!*

"So, are you going to tell me what happened between you and Lila last night? Because I in no way condone it." Kate groaned inwardly. Of course, her sister would not let her get off that easily.

*Condone this!* Kate shouted in her head. "Goodbye Im," Kate said and hung up, not about to get into any of that with her sister until she knew herself just what "it" was.

# 7

Jules, in her customary boxy, organic, stylish Mother Earth fare, sat on the edge of the white leather sofa, the same sofa that Lila and Kate woke on not two hours earlier. The woman's mouth slightly agape as Kate ran her through the events of the previous evening, well, at least the broad strokes.

"I need a joint," Jules finally said as Kate finished her tale. "Also, I need to let Luke know I'm gonna be a minute. Thank god I married a man who can parent." She cringed mentally as soon as the words were past her lips, knowing it was a sensitive topic on multiple levels for her friend.

Kate pushed at the fringe of red curls obstructing her view. "God, so do I."

"You're glad I married a responsible human that realizes the kids are at least half his fault or you need to smoke some weed?" Jules laughed, thankful her friend seemed unfazed by the comment. She knew Kate could get prickly about children, or her lack thereof.

Kate smiled back. "Both, seriously." It was such a genuine statement; Kate was in every way grateful both for the loyalty of her friend, and because one of them, at least, had found a partner that was just that, loyal in every way. Kate was jealous, of course, but more than happy for Jules and Luke, and she adored their kids. Every time they called her "Aunt Kate", she lit up.

"So, what are you going to do?" Asked Jules.

"I guess call Jenna and have some delivered," Kate said, only half joking, knowing that her assistant would be able to get her anything she wanted.

Kate pinched the bridge of her nose, willing the headache to go away. Wishing she could take back the last twenty years of her life and make all new choices. She'd felt like a sellout in her business for years, her husband left her for not one, but two younger women; an Instagram post with his hand on a much younger woman's ass was the start of their very public break up. The last thing she needed was a very public relationship with someone young enough to be her daughter.

Frankly, she wasn't sure she was ready for a relationship at all, or ever again. She could just move to Greece, paint, fuck a different cabana boy every day, explore ancient temples. She could practically taste the Ouzo on her tongue. It was a fine escape plan. Except, for the fact that she wanted Lila. They made love, they drank too much, they passed out tangled in each other. Kate remembered being happy for the first time in a very long time. Letting go of such joy seemed a terrible idea.

"I think I messed everything up, Jules."

The blonde shook her head. "Let me text someone, get something on the way. You, text that girl! I can tell you like her, and you are single!"

———

Lila's eyes went big as her phone vibrated on the table. "Oh my god, Kate messaged me!"

"You already have her number in your phone?"

Lila shook her head as she shrugged her shoulders, indicating that she was clueless; honestly not remembering how the number got there, but thankful it was.

Liz grabbed at the phone. "Is there a picture? Let me see!" She swiped at the message, "Oh," her eyebrows raised. "Kate Manderly," she said, reading the name above the text, "ho-ly FUCK! The Kate Manderly?" Liz's voice had gone up several octaves.

"Shit, you know her?" Lila asked.

"How were you an Art History major?" Liz handed Lila's phone back to her and started typing away on her own.

"You know I'm not into modern stuff."

Liz's eye roll was visible beneath the broad-brimmed hat. "Contemporary," she corrected, knowing Lila thought anything after 1900 was beneath her, and shoved her phone in Lila's face. "She's seriously famous!"

The photo on Liz's phone was sure enough Kate, in a classily low cut black dress, *Damn, she really does look good in black*, Lila thought, smiling widely in front of a step and repeat. Jealously flared in her; a man, Lila assumed Kate's husband, who, of course, was the definition of a silver fox, had his hand casually around Kate's small waist. He looked bored and unimpressed, while Kate looked radiant.

"Yeah," Liz said, noticing Lila's gaze, "total cliché d-bag. Basically traded on her name to become this hedge-fund guy, then goes after models that probably can't even put together a sentence just because they're twenty years younger than his still smoking hot wife. Who at least from what I've heard, is legit, one of the nicest humans on the planet."

Lila rolled her eyes. "Didn't seem so nice when she was booting me out of her place this morning," she grumbled. "And why do you know so much about her? You sound like a stalker."

"Okay, forgive me for paying attention to the world."

"Page six is not the world."

"Honestly, I'm surprised you even know what page six is, but hey, I'll take it. Kate Manderly is a brand at this point, literally. She signed all kinds of deals to put her work on purses, clothes, etc. Made a ton of money; made a lot of headlines, especially with her divorce. Guy was caught in a threesome on a yacht, of course.

As to her freaking out on you this morning, she and her husband were high school sweethearts, supposedly. I highly doubt," she motioned at Lila, "you were what she was planning on. Bold choice, though! It's going to put her work into a whole new context for me." Lila shot her friend a withering glare. "Also, did you read the text? She's totally into you," Liz grinned, "you have nothing to worry about."

Lila skimmed the message from Kate, her eyes widening as she did. "I feel terrible about my behavior earlier, so NOT a morning person. Can I make it up to you this afternoon? Drinks? I'd love to hear more about that restoration project you mentioned."

———

"There." Kate threw the phone to Jules and began pacing. "Happy?"

"Yes!" Jules said genuinely. "This is the first time you've shown any interest in another person in months! Or, ever! Well, not since..." Her voice trailed off, not wanting to bring up such an uncomfortable subject.

Kate briefly caught her friend's eye, but also had no intention of delving into that particular memory. "She's twenty-five! No, twenty-seven. Not that it helps at all! And." Kate paused, head in hand, "And she's a she! It's going to be all over the tabloids! And, oh my god, Wes!"

Jules rolled her eyes at the mention of Kate's ex-husband, but Kate went on. "Wes is going to have a field day with it! He'll be on some yacht somewhere laughing about it with the three twenty-year-olds he's fucking! Oh, God! Like I'm any better!" She groaned and plopped onto the sofa.

"Who cares about any of that?" Jules asked as she came to sit next to her best friend, putting an arm around her shoulders.

"You definitely shouldn't give two shits about what Wes thinks. The divorce is final; it's over. And you should know none of us care who you date as long as they're good to you; at least, not your real friends. Do what you want and be happy, and if the tabloids have a field day with it, so what? Honestly, I'm not sure what else they could drudge up."

"You know exactly what could come up," she shot back.

Jules' hands went up in defense. "Ok, ok, but you've been successful enough at this point to not care about what strangers think of you."

"If only that were true." She still found it stung anytime someone said something negative about her work or if she, god forbid, ended up on a worst dressed list, which, thanks to her current assistant, happened less and less. "I like men," Kate said flatly.

"Kate, I've known you since we were fifteen. You like beautiful things. Period. All of us know that, you aren't exactly subtle; you would practically drool every time Ms. Davidson walked in a room," Jules said of their eleventh grade Brit Lit teacher.

Kate snickered, "It was all that Byron and Keats."

"Please," Jules said, "I shared a room with you. I know what your brain did to that woman in your sleep."

Kate's face went red, but her eyes lit up and she grinned like the schoolgirl she'd been. "She did have the most amazing tits."

Jules laughed, nodding in agreement. "She did!" The topic could no longer go undiscussed; Jules would be remiss if Kate let this opportunity pass. She deserved to be happy, with whoever made her feel that way. Jules knew why her friend was hesitating; why she could never allow herself to be happy. It was the subject the two had danced around for the last fifteen minutes. "I also know about you and Cecile." Kate went cold at the mention of the name. "Don't let what happened there ruin this. Look," Jules said, trying to lighten the mood she'd brought down, "hang out, have a few drinks and scope out the situation. What happened with Cecile was a tragedy. I'm not telling you to marry the girl, yet. Maybe, like you said, you drank too much last night, had a fling, and that's that. But, maybe, you really had an instant connection with someone. Maybe this could be something amazing."

"Last time I thought I had that kind of connection, I wound up married for twenty years to a man who apparently never loved me."

"He was never worthy of you. Make sure this one is."

# 8

Lila went straight home from breakfast, feeling more sullen than excited. But she did, at Liz's insistence, message Kate back that, yes, she would let her 'make it up to her' later. She wasn't exactly sure what that meant. Liz was right about one thing though, knowing just who Kate was put things into a different context.

Kate wasn't just some bored socialite, she was someone, an artist, and she knew from her own temperamental nature just how volatile they could be. Liz told her that Kate must be interested in her, but now Lila wasn't so sure. She wondered if the invite this evening wasn't just Kate trying to placate her; make sure she didn't go to the press. Not that she ever would, no matter the circumstances.

That just wasn't who she was, but Kate didn't know that yet, and Lila, despite Liz's assurances that Kate was a decent human, couldn't fully trust her yet either. Probably never would get the chance now, Lila pouted inwardly.

At least she'd been able to get some rest after the much needed food, and, after yet another shower, she looked and felt almost human. Her phone buzzed as she was throwing a fitted black t-shirt over her head. It was Liz.

"What are you wearing?" she asked.

Lila looked around, half expecting her friend to be standing there. "Um, black t-shirt, jeans, some kicks. Probably bring a jacket."

There was a pause. "Ok, subtle, I'll take it."

"Thanks." What Liz didn't know was that it took her a good hour of trying on and throwing off one thing after another before finally landing on what amounted to her uniform.

"How do you not sound excited to be going on a date with Kate Manderly?" Liz was emphatic.

"Because I apparently, am not obsessed like you are."

"That's a lie. You are completely smitten!"

Lila blushed. "Whatever. I don't even know if this is a date. I just..." Lila's shoulders drooped, "I'm pretty sure I fucked everything up, and I'm pretty sure she won't date some random, who's also a woman when she's only been with men. Like, very successful men. I'm never going to be rich, or some important business person."

"Please, you're going to be on the cover of magazines as her boy toy, girl toy? I guess just 'girlfriend' works, in like a week. Also, you don't know you're the first woman she's been with. Unless, of course, she told you last night, which I'm assuming, you don't remember. So, deal with it. Also, good luck! I want all the details tomorrow, when you come up for air!" Liz laughed and hung up before Lila could respond.

Idiot, she thought, but smiled. *Kate's girlfriend.* The thought filled Lila with nothing but happiness; she cautioned herself though; she'd felt like that this morning and look where things ended up. Lila wrestled with her inner monologue and couldn't help but smile; yeah, they were ending up with her on her way to the Westside for drinks with Kate Manderly.

————

The doorman smiled and tipped a top hat as Lila approached Kate's building. "May I help you, miss?"

"Uh, yeah, I'm here to see Kate Manderly," she said, a bit nervously. Even though she'd been invited, she always felt like people looked at her like she didn't quite belong. Probably something to do with her mother's constant disapproval, or so her therapist theorized.

"Your name?"

"Lila Croft."

His eyes lit. "Ah, yes, Ms. Manderly told us to expect you. Please, go right on up."

Lila gave him a tight-lipped smile. "Thanks." Once again, she gave herself a once over in the mirrored confines of the elevator; subtle was right, maybe she should have put a bit more effort in. But, she noted with pleasure the way the black t-shirt highlighted her silvery hair and fair complexion; the tightness of her jeans showing the curve of her backside to perfection.

45

She was glad she hadn't overdressed when Kate opened the door similarly attired; oversized Rolling Stones t-shirt, worn cropped jeans, a flash of golden thigh peeking through a tear in the fabric.

Lila suspected Kate was the type that wore her jeans until they fell apart and actually picked up the shirt from a concert rather than a shop. The goddess-like curls that had fallen to her breasts the night before were pulled up into an artful mess atop her head, a few copper tendrils framing a quirked brow and smirk.

"Looks like we're in the same state," Kate moved aside and motioned Lila in with a nod of her head. "Hair of the Dog?" She asked as Lila followed her into the kitchen.

Lila grimaced, "So long as you don't mean whisky."

Kate gwauffed. "God no! Gin Lambruscos?"

"That'll always do," she said with a smile.

Kate smiled back and nodded in approval. "Good."

Lila watched as Kate moved around the large, stark kitchen; the faded jeans hugged her curves before loosening around the knees. They exposed her thin ankles and bare feet, her toenails painted a glossy midnight blue. Lila stood fixated as Kate brought out two thin stemmed glasses, a bottle of the Italian wine and a bottle of Hendrik's; she realized she could watch this woman do nothing all day and be happy.

She moved with such ease and confidence even though Lila was sure she could feel her staring a hole into the back of those jeans. Lila knew what was underneath them, and could barely think of anything beyond getting her hands back on

Kate's round backside. She felt a flare of heat in her cheeks at the thought.

Kate seemed so completely comfortable in her own skin, and that, on top of her striking looks, made her the sexiest woman Lila had ever been around. She still couldn't believe she was the object of Kate's desire, if in fact she was.

"Grab these," Kate said as she held the wine glasses and bottle out to her, startling Lila.

She smiled, "Sorry, you're pretty distracting."

Kate's eyes narrowed in contemplation as she tried to decipher the scene; she wanted nothing more than to apologize for her behavior that morning, but she wasn't a bit sorry for what had proceeded it. Well, she amended, perhaps they should have taken it slow. But then again, *no*. As Lila reached for the wine glasses and their fingers brushed against each other, Kate knew 'slow' would never have happened between the two of them.

Lila's eyes softened and a corner of her mouth rose as her fingers touched Kate's; she felt that same spark of energy Kate had, and her heart rate shot up. Her gaze took in Kate's mussed hair, the black bra strap peeking from the collar of her shirt, and those lips; those full, utterly kissable lips that seemed always on the verge of a grin.

"I'm sorry," Kate sputtered into the moment, and Lila found her sudden awkwardness adorable, even more so as it came from a woman who seemed so in control of every situation. "I panicked this morning," Kate continued, "and, I'd like to say I'm so sorry for that."

Lila took a deep breath and set the wine glasses back on the kitchen island, trying to steady her pulse, her hand finding Kate's and resting atop it. Lila found promise in the fact that Kate didn't pull away at her touch. "I hope, though, not for the rest of it?"

"No." Kate shook her head, but her expression was uncertain, and Lila wondered why. "I worry, maybe," she hung her head and her curls covered her eyes. "God," she started again, "do you feel I took advantage of you? Moved too fast? I'm a horrible flirt, but I've never been with anyone but my ex, I mean, not in a very long time and I've never just met someone and taken them to bed. You're marvelous, you know."

Lila relaxed, chuckled. If Kate's concern was whether she had been a willing participant in last night's activities, then there was only one thing to do to put her at ease. She wound her fingers through Kate's and brushed the curls from her eyes. "We never made it to the bed," Lila smirked, "but I would very much like to do so now."

Kate raised a brow, a mischievous smile playing in the corner of her mouth as Lila's thigh pressed against hers. "Yeah?"

"Yeah."

―――――

Kate lit the joint and took a long hit before exhaling, and passing it to Lila. "You know," Kate tipped her head to take in the late evening sun, light glinting off her overly large black sunglasses, "I'm not really as adventurous as people think." She paused and gave Lila a wan smile. "Well, at least as far as all this goes."

Lila nearly snorted as she laughed. "Could have fooled me!" She coughed, exhaling a plume of smoke.

The two spent the afternoon in Kate's massive bed and were now basking in the afterglow of their lovemaking; the sunset painting the sky a fiery pink as they lounged together on the large balcony, the river before them. Lila curled into Kate's side, finding comfort in her warmth as a breeze picked up.

"So, no kids?" Lila's gut clenched, even as the words were leaving her mouth. Was there any more emotionally charged question? *God, why bring that up? Why now? IDIOT!*

Kate sipped at her wine and shook her head. "Nope," Lila immediately picked up on the sadness in Kate's voice, "no kids. Wes didn't want any and honestly, at least for the first half of the marriage, I was too busy to give it much thought. By the time I did, well," she shrugged, "I'd been married to a man for half my life who made it very clear he had no desire for children. 'Un-tidy' actually, was what he called it; there just wasn't really any room for discussion." The sunset sparked off Kate's hair as she briefly turned away, and Lila noted the glistening of unshed tears in those green eyes behind the shades.

"But you could have them now," Lila smiled. She didn't know why, but all of a sudden, the idea of kids wasn't as terrifying as it had always been.

Kate laughed. "Please, I'm a bit ancient for all that."

"You are not! Women have kids into their forties all the time now."

"Yeah, geriatric pregnancies, they call them," she shivered, "adding insult to injury. God forbid you wait until you can actually afford a child before you have one, then you're called 'geriatric'!"

Lila grimaced before scooting closer. "They should really come up with a better term."

"Yes, they should."

"You're not old, Kate. You're forty-two, and you're the most beautiful woman I've ever seen."

"You're sweet," Kate smiled over her shoulder at Lila.

Lila brushed a thumb over Kate's lips. "No, I'm really not," she said and kissed her.

Lila could feel Kate roll her eyes, even from behind the glasses. "Lord," Kate said, a grin on her face, "hand me that joint."

Lila returned the smile, and after a hit, the joint as well. "Me neither, being adventurous, I mean," she took a stab at turning the awkward subject from kids, back to their previous track, "but people are always saying I look like trouble."

Kate was more than happy to leave behind the uncomfortable subject of children. It seemed like a random question, but one she supposed was valid if they meant to carry on; and she realized, she hoped they did. Her laughter calmed Lila a bit. "Trouble enough," she said, but there was a smile on her full lips as her arm went around Lila, pulling her more snugly against her. With that willowy yet curvy body, those penetrating hazel eyes, and, *that mouth*, Kate thought.

"The right kind of trouble?" Lila ventured.

Kate's green eyes appeared above the rim of her glasses, appraising her. "I suppose we'll see." She shook her head, curls bouncing around her face. "What the hell am I doing?" she said, but raised her hand to Lila's cheek, tilting her chin and placing a gentle kiss on Lila's lips. Lila smiled up into the bottle green eyes, and Kate laughed again, "trouble indeed," she said, draining her wine glass, setting it on the table, and turning her attention once more to pleasing and being pleased; their pleasured moans carried off by the wind.

# 9

Neither one wanted to go out; to leave the space that had, in such a short time, become their sanctuary. They'd decided on a light dinner, though both worked up quite an appetite after their many sessions of lovemaking. They ordered sushi and then went back to their exploration of Kate's bed and each other.

"So," Lila began, following their post dinner exploits, "I may have Googled your work."

"Oh, god. It's dreadful. Isn't it?"

"Are you serious?" Lila still wasn't sure where all of Kate's insecurities lay, but she couldn't believe she didn't know how very talented she was. She had to, she was the woman that built her art into a nearly billion dollar business. "I mean, you know Contemporary isn't my thing, but I can still tell good art from bad, and yours is very, very good art."

Kate gave Lila a seductive smile, her finger tracing a path along Lila's bare thigh. "You've already gotten me into bed you know, no need to butter me up."

Lila was a bit insulted. The last thing she wanted Kate thinking was that she was some sort of fan girl. She stopped Kate's hand with her own, holding it, waiting for Kate's eyes to meet her own. "Please don't. That's not who I am. That's not why I'm here."

Kate's chin dipped for a second, her mind racing. *How long has it been since someone wanted me just for myself?* She wanted desperately to believe that Lila was nothing but sincere, but she knew the ways of the world; she wasn't some kid fresh out of art school anymore. Kate knew that most people in this world only cared so long as you could do something for them. *Just try and trust her*, her inner voice chided her.

"I'm sorry," Kate finally said, giving Lila's hand a squeeze, "distrust sort of goes with the territory."

*Being famous? Being insanely wealthy?* Lila felt a wave of sadness for Kate. She didn't know which 'territory' Kate meant, but she got where she was coming from. It wasn't like she had grown up impoverished or anything.

In fact, she had a brother she hadn't spoken to in three years due to what he said were issues about money. So, Lila understood relationships were complicated enough without throwing money into the mix. She guessed fame alongside wealth added yet one more layer to be distrustful of people's motivations.

"I can't imagine what you've dealt with, the divorce, just people in general, I'm sure trying to use you. Please know I'm not one of them."

"Ok," Kate nodded, and Lila could see her eyes were glistening.

"Ok." Lila didn't want to pry, or seem like she was writing an article, but after she looked up Kate's work, she had to admit she was even more intrigued by this woman than ever. She was serious about not knowing pretty much anything about Contemporary art, other than what her art junkie friends told her, but like she had said to Kate, hers was top notch and she could understand why Kate was as well known as she was. There was something in her earlier pieces, though, that had made Lila wonder.

"If your work isn't an ok subject, I won't bring it up."

Kate sighed, but admitted to herself that maybe it would be different talking about her work with someone who was genuinely interested in her as a person; a fresh perspective, so to speak. She rolled over on her back, stared unseeing at the ceiling. "You want to know about the good stuff or the shit that's made me money?"

Lila tried to recall what they'd even been talking about; the tableau of Kate's nude form, lit by the Edison bulbs swaying above her bed, made it nearly impossible for her to regain her train of thought. She shook her head and smiled in bewilderment at her good fortune; the woman before her was beyond stunning. "The dark stuff," she finally managed.

Kate laughed again, and Lila realized it was something she did to hide her discomfort. "Not pulling any punches, are you?"

"I'm sorry," Lila shook her head; it sounded like a damn interview question.

Kate shrugged. "It's what made me famous, not what made me money, but I guess it's what brought me to the show, so to speak. The truth, not the bullshit story Wes conjured, the crap you'll find online; my parents died when I was twelve. I went to live with Imogen and her second husband; they'd moved to California by then."

Lila's brows furrowed, and her chest tightened with sadness for her loss. Before she could respond, Kate continued. "I was in the car with them when it went over." Her voice was thick with emotion, her eyes trained on the distant memory. "My father died instantly; it took my mother two hours; tree branch went right through her."

"Jesus, Kate," Lila breathed, her hand tightening around Kate's.

"I was told they found me the next morning, walking along the road, but I don't remember. I don't really remember anything until California; the blazing brightness of it. That's the light and dark you see, over and over. Painting seemed to be the only way I could get it out."

A single tear escaped down Kate's face, but Lila's own was wet with the cascade of tears she couldn't stop. In her mind, she recalled the photos of Kate's work online, the dozens of canvases, stark white with arcing black shapes.

"I'm so sorry. I had no idea."

"No one does. It's not something I talk about. Wes started telling everyone that my work had something to do with the darkness in all men, etc. You know, the sort of thing that gets you an article in the Times. It was the one time he protected me; I like to think he did actually love me in the beginning. Anyway..."

Lila could tell she didn't enjoy talking about it, that for some reason, talking about her grief made Kate feel self-conscious. Her own family was like that too. If they didn't talk about it, it didn't exist. Lila hated that, had spent years in therapy being assured by professionals it was ok to have feelings, to not be comfortable.

"It's alright to feel whatever you need to feel about that. You shouldn't be embarrassed about any feelings you have around me." She took a breath, making a leap. "I want to be your safe space."

Kate swiped at the lone tear, sniffled. Lila's words meant more than she could ever know, but she wasn't ready to go down that road yet and Lila could tell.

"Well," Lila said, attempting to steer them back onto safer ground, "I'd love to see your studio, see your work up close and personal."

"My best piece is right in front of you." Kate nodded to the painting on the far wall. Lila noticed it briefly earlier; she had been paying more attention to the woman in her arms though, than the darkly ethereal one in the painting at the time.

It was a stunning piece. "That's really yours?" Lila was shocked. It didn't look like anything Lila saw online by Kate.

"It is. Back from my college days."

Lila was out of the bed, wrapping a blanket around herself, eager for a chance to study the painting. Unlike the abstract works Kate was known for, her wide, fluid arcs, her use of negative space, this was a figurative piece. It was large, almost four feet across and six feet or more in length; a portrait. A woman, her dark hair almost lost in the Rembrandt like dark sky, sea swirling around her knees.

Her grey eyes stared out at the viewer, and one couldn't help but think she knew that the wave curling behind her meant to drown her, and that she did not care. It was a masterful work, combining the technique of the Old Masters with a brooding, apathetic tone that bespoke volumes of who Kate had been in those years. No one without an inner darkness could have painted such a piece.

Lila's hand instinctively moved to touch the painting, wanting to absorb the story it told, as if it could be imparted through contact. The professional art conservator in her stopped her though, just as her fingers were about to graze over the expert brushstrokes of a diaphanous white dress.

She felt the heat behind her as Kate pressed her body against hers, tucked her chin into the crook of Lila's neck. "It's ok," she said. "You can touch her. It's only priceless to me." Her tone was wistful.

The soft pads of Lila's fingers ghosted over the paint, feeling the tautness of the canvas beneath, feeling each stroke of the brush Kate made all those years ago. "Why don't you paint like this anymore?"

"No one paints like this anymore," she laughed rather wryly. "No money in it."

"I know how that goes," Lila whispered. "You know I'm going to ask who she is."

Kate sighed, "Yes, people always do when they know it's mine; there's more than one reason she's been in storage for so long. Wes wouldn't let her in the house, actually tried to burn her."

Lila pulled back to study Kate as she stared at the painting; this was more than just a painting to her. This woman meant something to Kate, or at least had at one point in her life.

Tears brimmed in Kate's eyes as she stared blankly at the swirls of paint on canvas; each brushstroke a memory. Lila felt Kate's sadness, though she wondered why she would keep a painting that upset her so much in her own room.

Lila turned and wrapped Kate in a tight embrace. It devastated Lila that she could ever cause pain to this woman. "I'm sorry. You don't have to tell me now."

Kate shook free of Lila's embrace, dropping to sit on the edge of the bed, "I'm scared," she said as her eyes met Lila's, "because I made the wrong decision before, and," she was crying now, "and someone died because of it, because I was too afraid to admit certain things to myself and I wasted all that time with someone who didn't love me. I'm terrified if I make the wrong decision again, that's it."

Lila stood before her, cradled her head against her abdomen. "The woman in the painting?"

Kate nodded.

"She loved you?"

"Yes."

"And you loved her?"

"I think I could have, if I'd allowed myself; if I hadn't been afraid of the feelings I had for her. But, I chose Wes. I chose to do the 'normal' thing; what I thought my parents would have wanted and expected of me. I was such a fucking child. And, well, things were different then. And I guess I was happy, for a time." She ran a hand through her hair. "Probably more blissful ignorance than happiness. I was such an idiot. And after," she paused, "well, just, after, Wes was all I had."

Lila was shocked, Kate had never said she'd been the first woman she'd been with before, and it really shouldn't have been all that surprising that she wasn't Kate's first, but that there had been such an intense relationship was a revelation. One which she wasn't ready to face.

"You always have yourself. Never forget that. And now, you have me, if that's what you want."

Kate grasped Lila's waist, pulling her closer. "I do want you! I can't remember ever wanting something so much! That's what scares me."

Lila disengaged, stood, holding out a hand. "Let's get some sleep. You've worn me out."

———

Lila was drifting, half asleep, her body heavy and warm; she could feel the neighboring warmth of Kate's body curled within reach. Physically, she was so at ease, yet she could not stop her mind from racing, an overwhelming feeling of contentment warring with the knowledge that they couldn't stay together in their happy isolation forever.

As she lay there, trying to untangle the joy she felt from the trepidation that was there as well, a cry from the other side of the bed bolted Lila upright. Kate was crying, deep, gut wrenching sobs.

"Kate!" Lila prodded her, and Kate rolled towards her, her eyes wide yet unseeing. Lila could see in the dim light, tears streaking her face. Kate mumbled something incoherent, and Lila prodded her again to no avail. She knew you weren't supposed to wake a sleepwalker, but she wasn't sure if the rules applied to someone having a nightmare.

"Cecile," Kate called in her sleep, the name the only intelligible words coming from her.

Lila squeezed her shoulder, shaking her gently, then more forcefully. "Kate! Kate, you're alright, you're just having a nightmare." Lila tried to make her voice as soothing as possible, but heard the fear that was in it as well; she'd never experienced a partner having a nightmare like this before, never seen someone in such pain in their sleep.

Kate came to with a start, an arm raised as if to strike at Lila. "Huh?" She sat up, shook her head. Lila could hear her trying to get her rapid breathing back under control.

Lila flicked the bedside light on. "It's ok" she said, "just a nightmare," she reiterated.

Kate looked around, still half asleep. "I'm sorry."

"Who is Cecile?" Lila asked.

Kate's eyes were red and her voice hoarse from the unconscious sobs. "Was I talking in my sleep?"

"You were crying."

"Shit, I'm sorry." She wiped at her eyes, trying to shake the dread from her mind. *Damn Jules for bringing her up,* she thought, though it was partially her own fault, she knew, for keeping her portrait of the dead woman in her own damn room.

"Kate?"

"Do we have to talk about this now?"

"Of course not. But, I'm here if you need me." Lila wrapped her arms around her, somewhat surprised that the other woman was allowing it, but happy she was; happier still, when Kate snuggled into her. Lila was worried. She didn't want to see Kate hurt, but she also didn't feel secure enough yet in their relationship to pry.

She didn't want to push. This was new and precious, and fragile? It didn't feel fragile; it felt shockingly solid. Even so, she felt cautious. So, instead of digging in, like she would have before with anyone else, she just whispered, "I'm not going anywhere."

The bed shook as Kate tried to control her almost silent whimpers. "I'll be ok, thank you," she said back, her voice thick with emotion and completely unconvincing. Eventually, the sobs turned to the slow breaths of sleep, but Lila lay staring, wide-awake, at the ceiling. *What the hell am I doing?* she wondered for the hundredth time since that first kiss.

# 10

Lila slept little after Kate's nightmare, not that she'd gotten much before the incident either, and now, as the early blue light of morning made its way into the bedroom, she found there was no use in her trying to sleep anymore. She kept turning the name Cecile over and over in her mind. Stared for what seemed hours at the space in the blackness of the night-darkened room where she knew the painting of the young woman in the waves hung.

She was trying to be as quiet as possible as she crept from the bed, pulling her t-shirt on over her head and tying Kate's discarded robe around her. She didn't want to wake Kate. After the strangeness of the early hours and Kate's clear distress, Lila was hoping to let her get some much needed rest.

She was yawning and rubbing at her eyes as she rounded the corner into the kitchen and... "Oh!" a petite brunette collided with Lila.

"Shit," Lila said, "sorry," too exhausted and distracted to be overly surprised.

The young woman whom Lila had just run into had gone into a slightly defensive posture, like she wasn't sure if she needed to attack or if Lila was going to attack her.

"Sorry?" She sounded English, snippy, and clearly peeved there was some unknown woman in a home where she clearly felt comfortable enough to have chucked her jacket and purse onto the white marble countertops. "Who are you?" She took in Lila's disheveled appearance, sleep mussed hair; she was wrapped in one of Kate's robes.

Lila grimaced, realizing she looked like she'd been up half the night having amazing sex, which she had. She held out a hand. "I'm Lila. I was just going to grab some coffee."

The other woman's eyes narrowed. "Where's Kate?" She questioned, ignoring Lila's proffered hand.

"Be nice," came Kate's sleep roughened voice as she shuffled into the kitchen. It seemed she had been telling Lila the truth when she'd said she wasn't a morning person; her hair was in a becoming disarray and she was actually wearing sunglasses as she made her way through the bright sunlit room. *Damn*, Lila thought, *must have woken her up!*

Kate lifted a hand, gesturing in the woman's direction. "Lila, this is my assistant, Jenna. Jenna, this is my friend, Lila. Lila spent the night last night. Now, can you please get the three of us some coffee before I have to go back to reality?"

Jenna's brows raised, but she gave Lila a tight-lipped smile and nodded to her boss. "Fine, but you know you have a very tight schedule today."

"I know, I know," Kate groaned and waved Jenna towards the coffeemaker, "but first, caffeine. Please!"

Jenna gave her employer an exasperated huff, but turned her back and began the day's tasks, starting with coffee.

"Working on a Sunday?" Lila asked Kate.

"Ugh, terrible, isn't it?" Kate smiled wickedly at Lila, put her hands on Lila's hips, and pulled her close. "What in the bloody hell are we doing?" She whispered, unbeknownst to her, echoing Lila's late night musings.

Lila wasn't sure how to act in front of Jenna, not that it shouldn't have been very obvious, she was wearing one of Kate's robes after all, and Kate's hands were on Lila's silk clad hips, nor had they done anything wrong, Kate was divorced and she was single. And if Kate didn't care about being open in front of her assistant, she didn't see why she should care.

"Does it matter?" Lila grinned up into Kate's beaming face, taking the other woman's lead, sliding her hand up the back of Kate's t-shirt.

Lila didn't want to see it, but Kate's expression faltered at her words; her lips pursing, a non-committal grunt accompanied by a quick nod of her head before she dropped her hands from Lila's waist and removed the sunglasses, placing them on the counter; her green eyes searching Lila's for any hint of betrayal.

*This isn't right*, Kate tried to tell herself. She was a very grown woman, going through a very public divorce, trying to get her life and career back on track. Questioning her sexuality and having a fling with a younger woman seemed the hallmarks of the mid-life crisis she'd been dreading and had accused her ex of not so very long ago. All she needed now was a convertible. *Wait, no,* she laughed internally, *I already have one.*

She had no clue just what this was or could be, or should be, for that matter, with Lila; she just knew she liked it and Lila very much. Despite that, no one wanted their heart broken, and especially not again, and not in public.

Jenna cleared her throat and held two mugs of coffee towards them. "Ah!" Kate said, breaking the tension; it was far too early in the day and she and Lila's hypothetical relationship to delve into such deep waters.

"You know we have to be at the museum in an hour," Jenna interjected into the awkward silence that settled over the three women. "And you look…"

"Eccentric?" Kate's tone was sarcastic as she smiled too brightly, knowing with her wild hair and swollen lips she looked like a well-fucked barmaid.

Jenna cocked an annoyed brow.

Kate shut her eyes tight. "Yes," she groaned, then nudged Lila with her hip. "I'm so old the Modern Museum wants to do a retrospective of my work; still fancy me?" Kate teased, a smirk playing in the corner of her mouth.

"Pretty sure I do," Lila said, returning the smile, desperately wishing Jenna wasn't there so she could show Kate just how much she did indeed 'fancy' her. Fancied the crinkles at the corner of her eyes when she laughed, fancied the way she somehow made the messy curls atop her head look like the sexiest thing on earth, fancied her mumbling in her sleep and soft little snores. Lila mentally face-palmed. So far, there wasn't one damned thing she didn't 'fancy' about Kate Manderly.

She wanted so much to wrap Kate up in a tight embrace, push her against the kitchen island, and feel their bodies meld as they had last night. But Jenna was there; would Kate's assistant be disapproving of their relationship or, god forbid, leak it to the press? Everything seemed so easy last night when it had been just the two of them, but now reality was sinking in just as she knew it must.

Kate seemed to sense the awkwardness of the moment. "Jenna, can you please be the amazing creature you are and find something that won't make me look ridiculous, or like I'm trying too hard? I'll be back in a minute, I swear!"

Jenna, who'd made a career of making herself unobtrusive, got the hint and said, "I'll do what I can," gave a tightlipped smile, and left Kate and Lila alone.

Lila relaxed at the assistant's exit; her fingers grazing over Kate's hipbone, tentatively as she closed the distance between them, reassured as Kate grinned and dipped her head for a kiss.

It was gentle at first, slow, neither woman fully accepting just how sure they were of the other, though at this point, there wasn't an unexplored inch of either. Kate ran a hand under the light t-shirt Lila was wearing beneath her robe, feeling the heat of the other woman's skin. Their kiss deepened, Lila groaned as Kate's tongue found her own, her hands finding purchase on Kate's round backside. The movement brought a groan from Kate as well.

It was Kate that broke the embrace, making a frustrated sound before brushing the hair from Lila's face. "I've got to get ready," she muttered through clenched teeth, need clear in the huskiness of her voice.

Lila nodded, frustrated as well, her nipples straining against the silk robe, her core throbbing; frustrated, but understanding. "I know, let me put on some pants and grab my stuff."

"Are the pants optional?" Kate teased, "You look so very good without them, unlike my fat ass."

Lila's jaw dropped. "Don't you dare talk about my favorite ass that way! It's perfect, if anything, I want it bigger," she grinned and was happy to see Kate blush. "And, while I would not be the first pantless wonder on the subway, I prefer not to need you to bail me out of jail after only one date."

Kate laughed. "Is there an acceptable number of dates before I bail you out?"

"Two, at the least!" Lila smiled and pecked Kate on the cheek before heading towards Kate's bedroom to retrieve her clothes.

Once Lila was dressed again, Kate followed her to the door. "That was lovely," she said, smiling.

Lila returned the grin. "I don't want to seem obsessed, but, any chance I can see you tonight?" She wasn't exactly sure where this was going, if anywhere at all, and she was trying very hard not to get her hopes up, but she thought, why not?

Kate hadn't wanted to seem forward herself, though she knew that sentiment honestly had already gone out the door; she thought it must be obvious how smitten she was, but she was glad when it was Lila that made the next move. "By all means," she replied, "be obsessed, but I guess not in a stalker sort of way," she laughed. "I'm slammed until this evening, but I'll let you know when I'm free."

"Sounds good."

Kate pulled Lila towards her and kissed her, "Until then."

# 11

It was drizzling as Lila left Kate's apartment to slog back to her own. She had to admit, New York was a different world from the thirty-fourth floor balcony of a penthouse. Her place was a fifth-floor walkup in the East Village with one window that had a charming view of an air shaft.

Pluses were that it was above a coffee shop and across from a ramen place, so there were advantages. But it didn't have Kate; a half hour without her, and already Lila was missing her. It was like she hurt when she wasn't in Kate's presence, and now there was an entire day to figure out what to do with herself. It was a strange feeling to suddenly feel so alone, without a particular person.

Her phone rang, and her heart leapt at the thought that it could be Kate; she was disappointed as she saw Liz's name.

"We still on for brunch?"

Lila ran her hand over her face, through her hair. "I'm a mess," she groaned.

"But in a good way, right?" She could practically see Liz wriggling her eyebrows suggestively.

"Jesus, Liz."

"So, that's a yes. I told you it was a date," Liz said happily.

Lila laughed, fumbling with her keys as she made it to her apartment. "Usually, I hate it when you're right, but I have to admit I'm glad you were in this case."

"Excellent! Brunch then? I can't wait to hear all about it!"

———

Jenna's brows raised as Kate entered her closet. "Yes," Kate said, "I'm seeing her, as in sexually."

Jenna made an exasperated, wide movement with her arms. "What? I mean, very obvious! You two were like bloody teenagers! But, what?"

"I shouldn't have to explain myself to you," she said, throwing off her t-shirt and grabbing at the green dress Jenna had picked out for her. She was on cloud nine and had no intention of letting anyone bring her down.

"You're totally right, but you're going to have to explain it to the rest of the world! It isn't fair, and it isn't right, but you know this is going to blow up in your face once it goes public."

"Why should it?"

Jenna gave her a look like it was exceedingly obvious, and Kate was being an idiot. She rolled her eyes. "I don't care. I honestly don't give a damn about any of that at this point. Wes got his when he left me, and he did it as publicly as possible," she said, referring to the revolving door of twenty-something influencers and models he saw fit to "date".

"Yes, and he has been very publicly shamed for it," which was somewhat true, to Kate's relief; it seemed the entire world hadn't lost what she thought of as decency. But where did that leave her? How was what she was doing with Lila any different? *Because of the way I feel about her*, Kate comforted herself. *It's different!*

"We aren't doing anything wrong! Unlike Wes, I'm not still married and carrying on an affair! And I want this to be an actual relationship, I think."

"No, you're not doing anything wrong, but I want you to be sure. You've only known this girl for how long?"

"Two days."

"Two days. We're planning the biggest show of your life over the next several months, and maybe this thing with you two works out and maybe it doesn't. But you can't let it overshadow everything else; your life's work. You know once this goes public, it's all anyone is going to talk about regarding you."

"I think I love her," Kate sighed. She knew Jenna wasn't wrong, that she needed to tread carefully with her heart, but not because she gave a fig about what anyone else thought, but because she'd only so recently had it broken.

Jenna stopped herself from yelling at Kate that she was insane, that, of course, she couldn't be in love with this girl that she'd just met; the sorrow in her boss' eyes made her soften. Jenna had worked for Kate for close to a decade and hated to see her hurt. She just wanted her to be happy.

"Just please, be careful."

Kate nodded. "I'll try." Jenna was right, it was true, her professional life had been moving towards this show. A retrospective at the MOMA was as big as you could get in her field. She knew she needed to focus on making this moment count, but she didn't want to let Lila go, either. There was so much to think about.

# 12

"You are glowing," Liz said as Lila joined her at their usual Sunday brunch spot.

"I keep getting scared I'm going to wake up," she said.

"So, I take it things went well. Did she apologize?"

Lila nodded, popping a bite of toast into her mouth. "She did," she said, grinning like the Cheshire Cat.

"You are so smitten!"

Lila felt the blood rush to her cheeks. Her friend wasn't wrong at all. In fact, Lila knew for certain that she'd never been so smitten in all her life. She felt giddy knowing that she could even feel this way about another human, much less that the person might feel the same towards her.

Her relationships thus far had proven to be one-sided. She was always trying to make things work, when really, the men she'd dated hadn't been all that interested in her. She did not understand whatsoever why Kate seemed to feel the same way she did, but; she was more than elated that it was happening.

"Are you going to give me the details or just sit there all smug?"

Lila thought about it, of course she wanted to tell her friend everything; how Kate felt in her arms, how it felt to feel so right in hers, how Kate giggled in her sleep; just thinking about that giggle was turning Lila on, how she cried, the anguish she it was not to be able to comfort her. But Lila wasn't an idiot. Now that she realized just how famous Kate was, she knew she had to protect her.

It wasn't her place, she felt, to talk about her, about them, in public, even if it was just to her friend. Truthfully, though, Lila realized, she wanted to keep all of it to herself, even if just for a little while. She hoped she wasn't wrong in thinking what she and Kate had was something special, and she wanted to keep this new and sacred piece of her life to herself for the time being.

Lila's fingers circled the rim of her champagne glass. "Everything is wonderful. She's wonderful and let's leave it at that for now."

"You're killing me," Liz said, but let it go. She knew Lila would tell her when she was ready, and she was the type that could respect that.

———

Jenna kept snapping at her to pay attention; it was no use, Kate couldn't think about anything but Lila. Her PR guru, a thirty-year-old named Kelli, was beyond frustrated. Kate apologized to them both, but she just couldn't focus.

She was trying to listen intently to the Director of the museum as she walked Kate and her entourage around, showing her the space they were planning on holding her show in. It was massive. She leaned over to Jenna. "Do I have enough work to fill this space?" She knew she did. Nevertheless, it was a wee bit intimidating.

"I don't know about good work, but certainly enough work." She was annoyed with Kate's distracted behavior, but understood it. Also, she was probably one of the few people on earth that knew just how shitty Kate Manderly's self-esteem was. Thanks to living with a man for two decades that constantly told her just how mediocre he thought she was while happily using her for his own gain. Jenna quickly said, "I'm just kidding."

Kate gave her a tight-lipped smile and nodded her head. She knew Jenna was trying to lighten the mood and had meant nothing by the statement. Despite that, it stung and put her in mind of the cutting remarks Wes would always make. She didn't want to think about her ex-husband, though. She wanted to think instead of Lila. Her lips curled in genuine pleasure at the thought of her; how she'd fallen asleep with the warmth of her curled around her, how Lila just stared at her and seemed to actually not find her wanting. How she'd felt totally herself in the other woman's presence.

She'd married Wes at twenty and had only had one relationship prior to meeting him; relationship was being generous. It was two teenagers groping at each other in the balcony of a church, of all places. Between Wes and the other boy, whose name had been lost to time, not one man ever looked at her with the same tender adoration that Lila did. No one, except Cecile, of course.

"Hey!" It was Kelli's brash Long Island accent bringing her out of her reverie, "sorry," Kelli was saying to the Director and photographer that had been in tow, taking 'candid' shots, "can we break for five? I need a word with our lovely and talented artist."

The Director smiled. "Of course," even she noticed Kate was off this morning.

Kelli said, "Thanks," and pulled Kate off to the side. "What in the fuck? You're the one who wanted to focus on your actual art and not your company, even though that's what's making you money, and now you're off in your head thinking about what?"

Jenna joined the duo. "She's met someone."

"Jenna!" Kate knew if she and Lila were actually going to make a go of it, Kelli would be the one dealing with the press, she'd have to know sooner than later so she looked more furious than she actually was as she felt the blood rushing to her cheeks.

Kelli perked up, her perfectly manicured blond brows raised in interest. "Well, now that is something!" She'd been Kate's press agent for years and had always genuinely liked her client. She'd been with her through the terrible, but much needed divorce, and now, she not only thought someone new would be just what Kate needed, but she also couldn't help thinking how the press of a new love interest of the famous artist would do nothing but boost her profile just in time for the announcement of her show.

"Don't get too excited, or start typing up the damn press release yet," Kate said, seeing the wheels of Kelli's mind already start spinning, "it's still extremely new and I'm not really sure how I feel about it."

"Seriously?" Jenna folded her arms, and Kate couldn't help but laugh at the seriousness of the accusatory glare on the tiny brunette's face. "You've been holed up with her for two nights, and I have eyes. I saw how the two of you were this morning. You weren't exactly trying to hide it!"

"Wait," Kelli interjected, "her? You've in a relationship with a female?" She lifted her arms and said, "Thank you," to the heavens.

"Oh my god," Kate grabbed at her arms, glancing over at the waiting Museum Director who was currently attempting, unsuccessfully, to pretend to be ignoring them, "the two of you stop it! It's a lot to figure out and I don't even know if she's ok with all of," Kate motioned to the vastness of the museum, to the photographer, to the two women beside her, "this. I don't want this to be a public relationship." The two other women gave her a non-believing glare. "What I mean is, I wish it could be just the two of us, like normal people."

"Ok," Kelli said, "well, you know you're not normal. No one worth over a hundred million is 'normal'."

Kate hung her head and sighed. "I know. Jenna and I had the same sort of discussion this morning. She wants me to make sure she's 'The One', or something before we go public."

"Good," Kelli said. "I'm glad I'm not the only one with common sense in your circle. So, obviously, I'd like to get ahead of this possible relationship, run a background check, etc, but," she took a breath, "you're my friend and my client. I'll take your lead on this and just let me know how you want to handle things." Kate nodded. "Ok, so, as your friend, I'm very excited for you and wish you all the best. Back to being your PR agent. I need you to pull your shit together for another couple of hours, ok?"

Kate smiled, "Ok."

# 13

After a few hours of brunching, Lila returned home, took a shower, then fell into bed. Champagne always made her sleepy, and after the past two nights, she was exhausted. When she woke to the sound of her phone buzzing a couple of hours later, she was at first confused, then as she saw the name on the caller ID, ecstatic; it was Kate, as promised.

"Hi," Lila answered.

"It's Kate," came a somewhat awkward sounding voice on the other end.

Lila laughed. "Yeah, I know."

"Oh, right." Kate face palmed. She'd never been this flummoxed around a man.

"So..." Lila realized this was the first phone conversation they'd had. She hated talking on the phone, and it didn't seem that Kate was any better at it than she.

"So, I just got finished up here at the museum; I told you I'd call." Again, she sounded like an awkward teenager asking a girl out on their first date. Bloody hell, she realized she was! "Um, would you like to grab dinner or something?"

Lila was ever so tempted to say, 'or something,' but went with, "We could stay in, if you want to? I didn't know if maybe you were too tired, or whatever," she finished. Falling right back into bed with Kate sounded like the most appealing thing ever, but she also didn't want her to think sex was the only thing she was after, because it wasn't.

Kate was torn. "I'd love to get out. Honestly, I've been cooped up in my place for far too long with take out and my own god-awful cooking, but..." she didn't know how to say what she wanted to; didn't know if it was even fair to ask. Lila knew who she was now, knew that most of her life was spent in the public eye, but knowing something and understanding it were two separate things. The last two nights had certainly been thrilling, and she'd connected to Lila in a way she hadn't with anyone else in a very long time. But was she ready to make this enormous change in her life public?

Thankfully, Lila picked up what she was getting at. "I know a dark little pizza place in the Village, I can promise no press and no unsolicited PDA's" She heard a sigh of relief at the other end of the line. She didn't know if Kate had been expecting her to pitch a fit or what, but she fully understood they'd been together for all of two days and if things blew up, neither one of them wanted to publicly deal with the fallout. If, and, she hoped when, they made things official, obviously things would need to change. But, for the moment, Lila was fine with things being just as they were.

"That sounds perfect. Let me run home and change. Just shoot me the address and I'll let you know when I'm on my way."

"Ok, I'll see you soon then," Lila said, "bye."

"Bye." Kate hung up, feeling the flush burning in her cheeks. She turned to see Jenna and Kelli watching her, indulgent grins on their faces; Jenna actually shot her two thumbs up before the two turned back to their conversation, leaving Kate on her own.

———

Lila whirled as someone touched her shoulder. "Wow," she said, taking in what she assumed was Kate's attempt at low-key disguise. "Never would have recognized you," she said in a teasing tone.

Kate looked excited. "Really?" She pulled nervously at the grey beanie that was failing in its attempt to cover her curls.

Lila held the door as she and Kate stepped inside. She laughed. "No, well, they might not know who they're looking at, but you're still the most beautiful woman here." Lila grinned back at her. Kate would be hard to miss, no matter what she was wearing, no matter where she was. She was a striking creature, with the wild mane of coppery curls, bottle glass green eyes, tall, built like a damn screen siren from Hollywood's golden era; even in a beanie and worn jeans, people would look; and they were.

Kate noticed it too. "Maybe we should grab a table."

"Booth in the back?"

"I'll follow you."

Kate's expression was one of pure bliss as she took her first bite of pepperoni pizza. "Mmm," she said after swallowing, "Do you know how long its been since I've had a real carb?"

Lila smiled, taking a sip from her beer. "You are gorgeous! I can't believe you worry about that shit."

"You will too once you hit thirty."

"No, my mom is one of those women that only eats salads; I've always found people like that to be the most miserable people on earth." Lila shrugged. "If going up a jeans size or two means I get to be sitting here eating food that makes me happy with someone who makes me more than happy, then it's worth it."

Kate laughed. "I like that philosophy. Wes always made me feel like I was a bad person, or weak, for not being as hard-core about that sort of thing as he was," she paused, "sorry, I don't want to be one of those people that goes on about their exes."

"We all have them; mine was an on again off again thing with the same guy since junior high. He showed up three weeks ago after disappearing for a year, then emails me and tells me he's sorry, but we're done and I won't be seeing him again."

Kate's chest tightened. She didn't want to be a rebound for Lila, or throw herself fully into this relationship if she was still in love with someone else.

Lila realized Kate was silent and reached for her hand. "Hey," she said, taking Kate's hand in hers, "that's been done for a long time, really; I needed a clean break to let go, and I got one. I'm not still pining after him or anything like that. I swear."

"But you loved him?"

"I loved the idea of being in love with him, even though we both never said we were serious but, now…" she trailed off, not knowing if she should be so forthcoming with her feelings or not. She didn't want to appear to be more serious than maybe she should be after only a few days of knowing Kate, but she also knew that she was in love.

"Now?" Kate prompted.

"Did you love Wes?"

"You're dodging the question," Kate's eyebrow raised in suspicion.

"So are you," Lila grinned back.

"Cheeky!" Kate winked. "I think we were so young when we got together, that it was the idea of being in love with him too; the fantasy of it; being married to your high school sweetheart and everything. I loved him enough." Even now, after her nightmare, she couldn't tell Lila the whole horrible truth. Not yet, if ever.

"I know how that goes," Lila smiled wanly. "But now, after being with you, what I had before seems so… I don't know… I don't know how to explain it other than, not real."

Kate's eyes softened, her posture relaxed. "What have we gotten ourselves into?" she asked, beaming at Lila.

# 14

Kate's finger stroked absentmindedly over the knuckles of Lila's hand; the moody notes of Coltrane's Lush Life drifted on the air from the record player, along with the scent of nag champa. Lila laughed when she'd seen the incense. "I use it for meditation!" Kate said defensively, not wanting to admit that every time she smelled it, it brought her back to those simple college days.

The moment between the two of them was a blessedly languid one, the two of them curled naked together on Kate's deep leather sofa, a mink throw pulled around them. It was the same sofa they had passed out on after that first lust fueled night; now though, Lila knew she was wanted, knew she was safe in her affection. Her head lay against Kate's chest, their every heartbeat in time with one another.

"Can it always be like this?" Lila startled herself with her words; she'd not meant to speak them out loud.

Kate rose up on her elbows, Lila raising her head to catch her expression as she rifled her fingers through the silvery locks of Lila's hair. "Are you sure about all of this?"

Lila's brows knitted together, "I've never been more sure."

"How's your mother going to take it?"

Lila did a mental eye roll. *My mother*, she thought, *she can get over it!* "Oh, she'll be in an absolute tizzy for a few days. Once she realizes our relationship won't hurt her social standing, she'll get over it. My father couldn't care less."

"I think that's the first time you've mentioned him. I haven't seen him in ages."

Lila gave a little shrug. "He still just sort of putts around and lets my mom tell him what to do and where to be when she wants to let him out."

"God," Kate said, "I couldn't live like that."

"Me either, but he doesn't seem to mind. I think my mom scares him, or it's just easier to let her get her way."

"People are funny, I suppose."

"For sure." Lila navigated the topic back to their imminent coming out as a couple.

"Does your sister know?"

"I think she suspects. She hasn't called you, has she?"

"No."

"Last time she called it was something about Wes of all people; she tried to ask about you, but I panicked and just hung up the phone," she laughed. "I've been dodging her calls ever since. I'm sure she's checked up on me via Jenna, but she wouldn't give us away; all Imogen needs to know is I'm alive."

"You two aren't close, then? Even after...you know?"

"Imogen was newly married when I went to live with her. She's far more British than I am; shipped me right off to boarding school. Don't really blame her for it. Plus, fifteen years is a big difference," Kate said, then realized what she'd said.

There was no use trying to minimize the difference in age between her and Lila, and she knew it would be a topic of conversation for the public, but mostly when it was just the two of them, it didn't even enter her thoughts. Until as now, it did; and at those moments, it seemed a glaring and insurmountable obstacle.

"I just feel as though I wasted so much time," Kate breathed, hanging her head.

Lila's heart stopped; it did every time she saw that broken look flash over Kate's features, leaving her looking like some wronged woman by Chasseriau. *Why won't you believe me that it doesn't matter?* She wondered desperately, un-wedging herself from Kate, standing, pacing as Kate watched.

*How do I show you I think you're the most magnificent creature on earth and I always will?* But Lila was no fool, and she knew what people would say; she didn't care. As far as she was concerned, she was getting the far better end of the bargain in a woman like Kate. Still, she understood how their age difference might reflect more harshly on Kate than herself; it was reality, stupid though it was.

86

"You're pacing. Is that a thing you do?" Kate's voice came to her from across the void of her thoughts.

Lila stopped, gently touched Kate's chin, tipped her face up towards her, meeting glistening green eyes with her own steady gaze. "Yes, it is. That time wasn't wasted," she said. "Now you can be sure of what you want and not let anyone else have a say. You're not a kid anymore, no one's wife, you're beholden to no one."

*How do you always know the right thing to say to me?* Kate swiped at the corners of her eyes. "No, certainly not a kid." She took a deep breath, let it out, holding Lila's gaze, *No*, she thought, *with you standing there, looking at me like that, I finally feel free.* "You're right. And, I know exactly what I want," she said, her mischievousness back on full display.

Lila yelped as Kate gripped her hips and tossed her back into the plushness of the sofa. How could she possibly be sad when they were together? Her body pressed Lila's into the leather, their fingers intertwining as Kate kissed a trail up Lila's neck. She didn't need time for the desire to build; she was almost always on the edge of it when Lila was near. Now, as her body fitted itself so perfectly over Lila's, as their lips met, their tongues entwining, Kate felt like to burst with the crushing need of it.

Her mouth broke from Lila's, her expression one of sheer pleasure as she gazed down at her, the perfect whiteness of her teeth biting into the fullness of her bottom lip. "Tell me you want me," Kate teased, the tantalizing weight of her breasts pressing against Lila's own more modest cleavage.

She looked up, Kate's hair a glowing red halo above her, framing her like the sultry Venus she was. "I want you," Lila was already breathless, every bit of her sparking with barely checked desire. She felt Kate's hand slide from her grasp as the other held firm, as Kate's body continued to pin her, Kate's hips pressing against her throbbing core. Hot fingertips traced over the thundering pulse at Lila's neck, the delicate bones of her clavicle. Her breath caught as they skimmed over the outer curve of her breast, the briefest pinch of a nipple to further tease.

Lila's free hand tangled in Kate's wild curls. "Minx!" Lila squirmed beneath her.

Kate's laughter was pure glee. "Just so." She released Lila's other hand, her body gliding against Lila's, causing her to shudder with anticipation, and her eyes squeezed tight as her breathing quickened. *Please*, Lila thought, *please*.

Lila felt hands spreading her already wet thighs. "God," Kate breathed, as the slickness of her lover met her fingertips. Kate's finger's found the sensitive nub, and rolling it, she smiled in delight as Lila whimpered beneath her. "You're so sensitive," she wondered, slipping her fingers inside, meeting the heat there; her thumb stroking in rhythm to her finger's pulsing.

Lila shuddered, whimpered with need again. "You should talk," she managed.

# 15

It was the third morning in a row they woke tangled up in each other, but the first time Kate had woken before Lila; she hadn't been lying when she'd said she hated mornings. But, she had to admit, she could get used to waking up to a beautiful silver haired, sylvan creature drooling ever so adorably on her silk sheets.

Kate didn't want to wake her, but she had to touch Lila, ever so gently, just to make sure she wasn't a dream. Her fingers swept the fringe from her eyes, trailing down the pale, perfect curve of her back, over the taught roundness of her backside, giving it a playful squeeze.

"Hmm?" came Lila's still sleep-addled response to Kate's touch. She smiled as her eyes opened to the vision of Kate naked above her. "Best thing to wake up to ever."

Kate sunk down on the bed, drawing one of Lila's nipples into her mouth. Lila's breath caught and her hips rose, pressing against Kate's weight.

She paused. "Let's see if we can improve upon that?" Kate winked, moved lower, her mouth pressing kisses along Lila's chest, her stomach, the tender flesh of her inner thigh. Lila's eyes focused on the red curls before her as her breathing grew stilted. Her hands found purchase in the tangle of Kate's hair as the other woman's mouth found her pulsing core. Lila whined as Kate's tongue circled, tasted, plunged itself into her, teasing, searching.

Her body was shaking, her thighs straining, every inch of her humming with need as Kate's fingers joined her tongue, the prior thrusting into her, their speed increasing along with her heart rate. Kate's eyes were squeezed tight as she thrust against Lila, who was writhing in ecstasy beneath her, soft moans mounting in volume.

Lila felt her entire body tighten; Kate was wondrous to watch as she strained against her, as her teeth bit deep into that kiss swollen bottom lip. Lila couldn't keep her hands from her; they felt like they were on fire as they slid up Kate's sweat-sheened skin, her thumbs brushing over her hard nipples, cradling her high, full breasts. Nothing in the world had ever felt so right in her hands, Lila thought; nothing in the world could ever feel more right than Kate did.

Kate's own moan joined Lila's and as Kate thrashed against her an exultant scream ripped from Lila's throat, her own body reacting to its partner's, shuddering, her fingers digging into the perfect, soft flesh of Kate's breasts, her own cry breaking around them.

Kate's fingers traced over the dark, delicate lines that covered Lila's ribs; the tattoo was a date in small, neat lettering. "What's this date?"

"When I got my Masters; kind of a 'fuck you' to all my teachers back in California. They didn't think much of me." She shrugged like it meant little, but Kate could see that wasn't the truth.

"Mine didn't much like me either. Called me lazy, difficult to teach," she rolled her eyes. "I was just bored and wanted to learn so much more than what was in those sterile textbooks."

"Gah, me too!" Lila lit up. "They acted like because I wasn't interested in calculus I must not be very bright, when I was spending all my free time reading history books and biographies of the Old Masters."

Kate rifled through Lila's hair. "Glad you're not still bitter," she grinned playfully, and Lila swatted at her arm.

"Yeah," Lila said, "you either." She laughed, and Kate cocked her head at the sound of it.

"What?"

"Nothing."

Kate's lips pursed. "It's something, tell me."

"It's just funny that here you are famous, brilliant Kate Manderly, and you're still pissed about high school."

Lila watched a shadow cross over Kate's features, her eyes go hard. "Wretched place," she said, clearly disgusted.

"What was the teacher's name?" Kate arched a brow and Lila wheedled, "Whoever made you hate school so much that even now you look like that when it's mentioned."

Kate took a deep breath. "Mrs. Schwartz; terrible woman, math teacher. Actually made me cry frequently. I used to sit there, imagining I'd find her house and throw a brick through the window."

Lila laughed loudly at that, wrapped her arms around Kate and gave her squeeze. "Such a little rebel." She didn't want to move, to break the closeness of this moment. Her fingertips played over the bones of Kate's spine as they both lay still. "How is it Monday already?" Lila groaned.

Kate raised her head. "Back to reality, eh?"

"Yeah, just me and Caravaggio. And lots of coffee."

"You're going to have to invite me to work one day, you know."

"I'm not sure you need me to get in," Lila teased. Both knew full well that if Kate Manderly wanted to get into the back rooms of the Met, all she had to do was ask.

Kate sighed, her fingers stroking down Lila's arm. "I wish we could just stay here all day."

Lila grinned, placed a kiss against Kate's forehead. "Me too." She reluctantly left the warmth of the bed, found her jeans, slid them on, shrugged her shirt on after.

Kate looked amused. "You know you can shower here. We have hot water above 14th street."

"I know. We have," she said, recalling several delightful moments the two of them had shared in Kate's massive shower, "but, I mean, I don't want you to feel like I'm presuming too much."

Kate rolled onto her stomach and the sight of her nude form in repose was, yet again, making thought difficult. *Seriously,* Lila thought, *the woman doesn't have a bad angle!* "You can presume anything you want at this point," Kate grinned. Lila laughed, shaking her head as Kate stretched in obvious invitation, Lila knowing that Kate knew just how beautiful she was in the morning light.

"I'll have to take you up on that another time. Our little morning delight is going to make me late as is, and I know if I get in that shower of yours with an endless supply of hot water, I'll never get out."

"Suit yourself." Kate watched Lila finish dressing, shocked by the realization of how lonely she felt by the thought of being without the other woman, even if just for a few hours. Lila caught her watching, smiled, came back to sit on the edge of the bed. She reached out a hand to card through the wildness of Kate's mane. "Believe me, I've zero desire to go back to real life."

"This could be real life, you know." The words were out before Kate had time enough to think of their consequences.

Lila's heart leapt in her chest. She had known since day one that this creature before her was her everything; that she would never feel the same way about another living soul. But was it too soon to get this deep? Of course, every successful couple she'd ever known had said the same thing; it was like lightning, they just knew, etc. Knowing the person for an hour or a year wouldn't change their feelings.

Lila was sure that's what had happened with Kate, at least, on her part, but did the other woman feel the same? She had to, didn't she? They'd spoken about their relationship at some length last night; about the fallout. The love that Lila was sure was there, though, had remained uncommented on.

Kate spoke again. "Just promise me this is real, not just some infatuation. Lila, I want to be with you. Just you." She seemed embarrassed; her tone and the blush creeping up her cheeks, totally at odds with the wantonness of her pose. "I'm a loyal, romantic sort. And, despite the swiftness of our relationship, I promise you, I don't bond quickly. I don't trust easily."

Lila had a sly, teasing grin on her face. "Are you asking me to be your girlfriend, like, officially?" It was a moment of truth and both of them knew it; if they made this decision to be together, to be in public together as a couple, their lives would change.

Lila's hand took hold of Kate's hand and together with her own, she placed their two hands above the rapid beat of Kate's heart. "It's safe with me. I promise."

Kate smiled in response; tears glistening in the corner of her eyes. "I know. I have no idea why, but I know. I knew that as soon as our eyes met in that first moment at the party. Fifty other people in the room and they all disappeared for me. You were the only thing I could see; the only voice I could hear. I've never felt that before."

"Me either, except every time I'm with you."

Kate blushed even more deeply, matching the color that bloomed on Lila's cheeks as well. "We keep carrying on and it's going to be public knowledge very soon; it may as well come from us."

"I don't want this to ever end."

"Neither do I," Kate agreed, pulling Lila down into a kiss.

Lila broke from the embrace. "Sooo, I am your girlfriend?"

Kate laughed, swatting at her rear. "Yes! You're my girlfriend. I'm going to have to tell my PR firm today; I'm too damn old to be sneaking around the East Village."

# 16

"Gah," Lila dropped her bag to the floor, unceremoniously thudding against the black herringbone, feeling for the first time like she was coming home rather than just being a guest at Kate's apartment. "That was the longest day of my life!" She groaned as Kate came into view.

Kate's sunglasses were still on as she crossed the living room towards Lila; she'd spent the day absorbing the last of summer's warmth on her patio, doing her best to pretend that life was about to be anything other than hectic.

"Does that mean you mean you missed me?" Kate grinned, wrapping her arms low around Lila's waist, pressing a quick kiss to her lips.

Smiling hazel eyes gazed back up at her. "Maybe a little," she teased, pushing Kate's glasses back up into her pile of curls so she could see those green eyes. She twined her fingers through Kate's and tugged her through the foyer back to the living room, pulling her down to the sofa, Kate chuckling the whole way.

"Someone's eager!"

"I'm dying to know! What did Kelli say?"

"Ah," Kate said in understanding. She may have spent her afternoon in the warm glow of an early autumn day, but her morning had been all about the business of being in a new relationship which was about to be front and center in the very public eye. Kelli spent close to an hour just going over what the ramifications could be. "As a friend she said, and I quote, 'get some,' as a publicist, she thought we should be seen out and about together for a week or so before making it publicly official.

A former intern of mine is having his debut show in a week; I was planning on going and Kelli agreed it would be the perfect place to be seen together, as a couple for the first time. Nothing over the top, you know, just being us, and I'd be amongst friends." She squeezed Lila's hand, hoping she wasn't as nervous about the whole thing as she was.

Kate had been in the spotlight for close to twenty years, but she never managed to get used to it; never understood why people cared about what she did, what she wore, who she loved. But they did; she just prayed Lila was up for it.

Lila groaned. "And I thought today was a long time, a week of not being all over you at all times is going to be an eternity!" She grinned, fingers trailing up the back of Kate's neck. "How am I supposed to keep my hands off you in public?"

"Well, you managed the once."

"Barely!"

"I hope you know it's just as hard for me," Kate said, her hands running up the back of Lila's jean clad thighs.

"It better be!"

Kate bit her lip, eyes raking over Lila, taking in the full, parted lips, the nipples pebbled beneath the thin fabric of bra and t-shirt, her thighs splayed atop her. "I assure you it is."

# 17

That night they kept it casual, hitting a noisy brasserie in SoHo, just as Kelli suggested. Kate hadn't been seen out and about since her split, so there was a bit of buzz, but as she seemed to just be out with a friend, it was the manageable sort. The two had a few glasses of wine, dinner, made mundane small talk and, as planned, Kate's car dropped Lila at her place before taking Kate back uptown to hers. They hadn't been apart for a night since they'd met.

*What are you wearing?* Came the text from Kate, even as Lila was turning the deadbolt to her apartment. She laughed as she saw her screen; it had been less than five minutes since they parted.

She threw her bag onto the sofa, grabbing a sparkling water from the fridge and plopping herself down on the worn leather cushions. *Black silk negligee,* she typed, grinning. *The highest of high heels, sipping on the dirtiest of martinis. U?* She pictured Kate laughing as she read the obvious tongue-in-cheek reply.

*Nothing,* came the quick reply.

*Alan's wife will not be too happy about that,* she wrote back, referencing Kate's driver. Kate sent back a laughing emoji, *Wish you were with me.*

*Me too. Soon.* Lila typed, added a heart, and turned on the shower. There was no way she was going to get much sleep tonight thinking about Kate, all alone in her bed, without a doubt in the nude.

They were out and about together again the next night. This time it was a saké bar downtown, followed by ramen. It was a night of more small talk, more trying their best not to get too close, not to look like they were in love. But the night had turned cold, and the saké did just enough to lower their guard.

When they left the restaurant, it was Kate that silently slipped her hand into Lila's and, ever so briefly, pulled her close.

Lila was shocked, having been very conscious not to make any moves that could be seen as romantic in public; she was trying to respect Kate and Kelli's relationship rollout plans, after all. But, if Kate made the first move, could she make the second, she wondered.

"Will you come home with me?" Lila whispered as she pulled on Kate's hand, bringing her closer.

Kate smiled, bent her head towards Lila's; a group of college kids brushed past them, heading down the stairs to the subway, and Kate seemed to remember where they were; a street corner in New York where anyone could see them. She dropped Lila's hand and stepped back; looked around, and, pleased by their apparent solitude, said, "Let's get a cab."

The last remnants of summer storms were threatening the city but hadn't broken yet, so it took only a few minutes to hail a cab. As they scooted across the vinyl seats, Kate's fingers grazed the tips of Lila's, and she looked up. Lila said they could just walk; the image of kissing Kate in a rainstorm flashing in her mind, but she could tell Kate was still unsure of being seen with her and so had acquiesced to the ride.

"I know you're frustrated with this," Kate started. She saw the annoyance flash across Lila's features. The cab driver was chatting away to whoever was on the other end of his earbud, clearly not paying any mind to the two women in his backseat.

"It's hard for me, too. I know I said that before, but, I hope you know that." God, how Kate hoped Lila knew. Yes, there would be talk and snide articles, but she'd have a partner she could be herself with and to her, that was worth everything else, so long as Lila was really who Kate hoped she was.

Lila wanted to reach for Kate, but the night was suddenly claustrophobic; the sticky bench seat of the cab, the incense wafting from the front, the cloying heat of the airless city. It was all too much for Lila, and she struggled to roll down the window.

"Are you alright?" Kate asked, even though it was clear Lila was not as she started dry heaving, her hand covering her mouth.

"Pull over!" she gasped, flinging open the door and heaving onto the sidewalk as the cab screeched to a halt.

"Oh, my god!" Kate slid across the bench, threw some bills into the slot of the cab's divide, and helped steady Lila as she stood shaking, propping herself up against a filthy brick wall.

Lila caught her breath, felt her stomach calm as her nails scraped against the crumbling brick mortar. "I'm fine," she said weakly. *God, how embarrassing*, she thought.

Kate glanced around. It was getting late and the street was empty. "You're not fine." Her voice was stern and full of genuine concern. "How far are we from your place?'

"Next block."

"Can you walk?" The cab had, of course, already sped off.

"Yeah, I just got overheated. Really, I'm ok. Let's go."

———

"I'm going to have to start doing cardio again," Kate called from the tiny bathroom as she ran a towel under the faucet, wringing it out and picking her way back through Lila's dimly lit apartment. It had been quite a while since she'd found herself in one of these downtown walk ups; she still found them charming, so long as the stay wasn't permanent. But she was worried about Lila.

She hoped how she'd acted back outside the restaurant wasn't behind Lila's sudden illness. She didn't enjoy being this paranoid person, constantly looking over her shoulder to make sure a telephoto lens wasn't about to capture her doing god knew what. But it had become the reality of her existence.

Despite her queasiness, Lila smiled into the shadowy room. The image of her darling uptown Kate, schlepping her up five flights of stairs, a memory she would cherish. Kate had, not complaining once as, shoulder under Lila's arm, they climbed the stairs to her apartment.

"Here you go." Kate stood over Lila as she lay on her battered leather sofa.

She smiled wanly up as Kate placed the cool towel over her forehead. "This is so embarrassing."

Kate plopped down beside her, pulling Lila's legs up over her own. The casualness of the action shocking and pleasing both women. "I went to college you know; hardly the most embarrassing thing I've seen, or the first girl I've carried home." Lila's brows raised, and she lifted her head in question. Kate shook her head, laughing at the misunderstanding. "You'll have to meet my friend Jules," Kate elaborated, "whisky sours were not her friend."

Lila grunted and sat up. "I'm feeling better, thank you," she said, shifting under the weight of Kate's legs.

"You're welcome?" Kate said in a questioning tone, hoping terribly that she wasn't being dismissed. She wished she wasn't in a state of constant panic that she was going to do or say something that might run Lila off.

Lila, sensing her tension, cocked a brow and ran a hand over Kate's, "As much as I love you on top of me, I'm going to have to get up and brush my teeth before I kiss you, and I very much want to kiss you right now."

"Oh!" Kate was beyond relieved. "Of course! Let me help you up!"

———

"What?" Lila's head shot up as she heard a phone ringing. She was tangled up in sheets and one unconscious redhead. The phone continued blaring. She rolled to one side, dislodging Kate, who groaned in disapproval. It wasn't Lila's phone ringing. Hers was silent, but as she picked it up, she saw several missed calls. *What the hell?* It was six o'clock in the morning!

"Kate?" She nudged at the sleeping form beside her.

"Hmm? What is it?" Kate asked, flinging an arm to shield her eyes from the non-existent light. "What time is it?" She said, chancing a look around with one eye.

"Your phone is ringing!" Of course, by that time, the ringing had ceased.

"No, it's not," she grumbled. The light and blaring tone of an air-raid siren started back up. "Bloody hell! Alright!"

"What in the hell, Jenna?" Kate yawned into the phone as she answered. She was silent for a moment "Good lord!" She smacked at Lila. "Twitter! We're on the bloody Twitter!" Kate was silent again, listening to Jenna; Lila could hear the tiny Brit's loud barks from the other end. She hurriedly swiped at the numerous alerts on her phone messages from her mother, brother, Liz. Her stomach dropped as she tapped on her Twitter app.

There they were, Kate's hand in hers, Kate leaning in; the photo captured the exact moment where Kate's forehead had ever so briefly touched hers. It was an intimate moment between two people who could have been nothing if not lovers.

Lila's hand, unbeknownst to her, was brushing the back pockets of Kate's jeans, their hips and thighs pressed against each other. How had they not realized how obvious they were? And now, they weren't just on Twitter; they were trending. *Fuuuck!* She thought.

Kate, still silently taking her verbal beating, motioned for Lila to show her the photo; she glanced at the brightly lit screen, the only source of light in the predawn dark of Lila's bedroom. Kate took a deep breath, shut her eyes, then tilted her head back before nodding in agreement with whatever was being said on the other end of the line.

"Alright," her voice was barely above a whisper and Lila could hear the tears held back in it. "Alright, I'll call you back," and she hung up without a 'goodbye', plunging the room back into darkness.

Lila held her breath, waiting for Kate to break the silence. When no words came, she fumbled for the bedside light, flicking it on; that got a reaction from Kate, who dove under the covers.

"Kate, are you alright?"

"Of course I'm not alright!" came her muffled voice.

Lila lifted a corner of the comforter, spying a wide green eye. Kate's hand darted out and pulled the comforter back over her head. Lila couldn't help but giggle at the childish antics. "Ok, but, we already decided we were going to go public in the next few days; it's not that big of a deal, is it?"

Kate sat up, pulled the blanket from her head and fixed Lila with a withering glare. "If we aren't in control of the situation from the start, it's going to get out of hand."

"Is that Jenna or Kelli talking? Because it doesn't sound like you. This isn't exactly the first time you've been in the press, nor is our relationship the end of the world. I thought this was what we wanted?" Lila's phone started buzzing again and again. It was a call from her mother.

Kate tried to slow her breathing, bring her heart rate down. "I just wanted, for once, to do things on my terms."

"Our terms, you mean?" Lila prodded, and she saw Kate pause, look at her, the reality of the situation not just for herself, but for the woman she loved as well, coming clear.

Kate clutched at her hand and gave her what she hoped was a reassuring smile. "I'm sorry. I'm being a selfish idiot! I don't like it, but you're right, this isn't my first time around; but it is yours. Are you alright?"

Lila gave her hand a squeeze back, "So long as you don't leave me in the lurch."

She smiled, dropped a kiss onto Lila's forehead. "No intention whatsoever," Kate said, her voice returning to its usual low and teasing tone. Kate's phone buzzed; a text from Jenna. "Press is outside, she says," she turned back to Lila and gave her an overly bright smile, "looks like you're well and truly stuck with me."

"I'm not complaining. I knew this was part of being with you," Lila tried to reassure her.

Kate groaned and slid from the bed. "Well," she said, as she searched for her discarded clothes, "if we're going to do this, I best start some coffee."

They had coffee, then more coffee, then realized they were going to need backup and also more than the leftover pizza in Lila's fridge. Kate decided it was time to call in the professionals.

"Lord," Kate gave her reflection more than a once over; it was not a pleasing sight; the greenish, buzzing fluorescent overhead lights in Lila's cramped bathroom, not helping. "I look like death warmed over. I can't possibly go out there looking like this."

"You do not!" Lila sidled up behind her, wrapping her arms around her and admiring the woman in the mirror before her. "I've never seen someone who carries themselves with such confidence have such low self-esteem. How do you not understand how gorgeous and sexy you are? I mean seriously, it takes everything I have not to just try to keep you in bed all day."

Kate quirked a brow at their reflections, her, with her hair sticking out in all directions, clothes rumpled from half a night on the sofa, no makeup. But then, she saw the way Lila was looking at her, and she grinned, blushing, shaking her head. "You're ridiculous," she said, but couldn't help but feel almost overwhelmed by the joy within her. How long had it been since Wes had looked at her that way? Since anyone had?

Lila's smile matched Kate's as she saw her light up. "There it is," she crooned. Kate's blush deepened; she was trying in vain to wipe the stupid grin from her face. "You totally love me, don't you?" Lila said.

"Oh, shut up!"

Twenty minutes later Jenna showed up, bagels in one hand, a small duffle and a garment bag in the other. "You're a life-saver, Jenna!" Kate said, pulling the younger woman into the apartment.

"You two," Jenna began, "are hell on my personal life." She held the bag of bagels out to Lila, who immediately tore into them; the duffle bag, she handed over to her boss as she tossed the garment bag over a chair.

"What personal life?" Kate quipped, not meaning it. She knew her assistant had always gone above and beyond.

"Exactly," Jenna replied.

"It's very much appreciated, and you know you'll be well compensated."

Jenna looked around the tiny, dimly lit place, absolutely appreciating just how well compensated she was; she could afford a place with an actual window, a street view, in a building with a doorman. "Don't I know it."

Kate gave her reflection a last once over, sighing; it was as good as it was going to get without a stylist and professional makeup artist. She wasn't one of those celebrities that went about her daily life being "crewed" every morning, but when she knew cameras were going to be on her, she had to admit to being vain enough to want to look her best. *Bless Jenna though*, she thought. She had done her best, and she looked, if not polished, at least well groomed and rested in a clean outfit.

Lila, on the other hand, looked like she'd been caught on the street by a fashion blogger, lilac hair artfully tousled, framing her sculpted face; her leather jacket over a printed silk button down and wide cut trousers. It was the most put together Kate had ever seen her, and she couldn't help thinking the most nervous, too. She gave her a small smile, pulled her close, their foreheads meeting as they had in the now famous photo. "We're going to be alright."

"The two of you should leave together," Kelli was telling them through the speaker of Jenna's phone, "otherwise, it's going to look like a walk of shame by whoever leaves first."

"Already done that once," Lila said, Kate grimacing as she recalled throwing her out after that first night. The memory of her atrocious behavior, Kate knew, would never cease to sting.

Kate gave Lila's arms a squeeze in both apology and acknowledgment. "I assume the car is waiting out front?" she asked Jenna, who nodded in the affirmative.

"I know it's a bit much, but we can drop you at work," Kate suggested.

Lila laughed, "Yeah, it would suck to miss the subway."

"That's a great idea!" Kelli piped up from the phone. Lila sighed, knowing she had little choice in the matter if she wanted things to go smoothly, which she did.

"Fine!" she gave in, throwing her hands in the air. Lila wasn't furious, just annoyed, she didn't want to be famous for being someone's girlfriend; she didn't want to be famous, period, but here she was at 8 AM planning her day according to what would trend most positively with key demographics on fucking social media. Lila thought she'd be ok with it.

She'd thought she had mentally prepared herself for the ordeal that went along with being a celebrity's partner, but all her planning and thinking things through didn't come close to the reality of the situation. It was worth it though, she kept telling herself; *Kate would always be worth it.*

Kate could tell she was spinning. "Jenna," she said, "could you give us a moment?"

Jenna turned around the small one bedroom studio. "Where am I supposed to go?"

Kate fixed her with a look and Jenna, being an intelligent human, took the hint, picking her phone up off the coffee table. "We'll call you back Kelli," she said into the device, pressed "end," and was out the door.

"I'm not alright," Lila managed as the lock clicked shut behind Jenna. Her eyes were wide, her breathing quick.

Kate sighed, wrapped her hands around Lila's wrists, fixing her with a stare. "Just breathe, love."

Lila tried taking a deep breath; her chest was tight, the sound of her pulse thudding in her ears. Her hands were shaking with anxiety as Kate grasped them in her own. "I don't know if I can do this," Lila's voice was strained with emotion; the last thing she wanted to do was disappoint Kate.

"Please trust me," Kate planted a delicate kiss on her forehead, her lips. Her eyes pleaded with Lila. "Please. I'm not going anywhere. I'm in this right beside you."

# 18

They stepped out of the little painted brown metal door of Lila's walkup, hand in hand, and just like that, they were official.

Lila was nervous about what she feared was going to be a great deal of scrutiny and judgement, not only from the public, but her friends and family as well; her mother especially. No matter how much she loved Kate, and Kate loved her, she still had to stand on her own because Kate wasn't always going to be by her side with a reassuring embrace.

The original plan for the rollout, so to speak of their relationship, would have at least afforded her a weekend to deal with the fallout. Now though, as the Mercedes' door shut firmly behind her, the realization that she had to get through this day on her own became clear.

As expected, Lila's mother called about two minutes after the "leaked" photo of the new couple showed up on a famous blogger's Twitter, and the calls kept coming, but she didn't answer. By the time Lila decided to finally pick up one of those calls, it was late afternoon and she'd snuck away to eat a sandwich in the park, away from prying eyes.

"When were you going to tell me you're a Lesbian?" came Janet's panicked, pinched voice from the West coast.

"Jesus, mother, how have your sleeping pills even worn off yet? And you have no idea what the password to your computer even is, much less Twitter; who called you?"

"Your brother."

"Oh, that's a reliable source!" Lila was furious; no one could set off her rage like her mother. Well, her mother was a close second to her "little" brother.

"Is it true? Because I've had about ten phone calls in the last twenty minutes alone, not to mention the one from you brother waking me up at three o'clock in the morning! I've been trying to reach you for hours!"

"I've been more than a little busy, and yes, it's true," Lila sighed into the phone. She wanted to tell her mother that it was none of her business, but she suddenly felt too ill to even care about her disapproval. She took a deep breath, feeling her mouth start to water as a wave of nausea overtook her. "Mom, I have to go," she said quickly before hanging up and laying back on the grassy hillside, trying to keep the bile at the back of her throat from spewing. These nerves, it seemed, were getting the best of her.

Lila put her phone on Do Not Disturb. The day finished up with no further illness or panicked calls from her mother, and she found herself relieved to be standing at Kate's door at the end of her long day.

Lila actually welcomed the push and sway of the subway that evening on the way back; how not a single person took any more notice of her than anyone else. No direct eye contact; in this way, being in New York was a blessing. Anonymity was possible in the city.

She'd had no such luck though as she made her way past security and into the bowels of the museum that morning. There were only a handful of people in her department, a few interns; they all stopped and looked at her as she entered. Her face felt like it was on fire and she suddenly had flashbacks of the misery that was lunch in the high school cafeteria. Ugh, she thought. It had been an endless day.

"So..." Kate wheedled Lila as they walked out onto her balcony. "How was work?" Lila's first day of being a celebrity girlfriend had certainly been an experience.

"You know that dream where you show up in class and there's a test you didn't know about?"

Kate's face was one of amused adoration. "Well, I'd say it's been a great deal longer for me since I've been in school, but, I see your point." She grinned and wrapped her arms around Lila, reveling in the feeling of their bodies pressed tight together.

"All damn day people were just staring at me, except of course for the lone intern who asked if I could get her your autograph because you're 'like, her hero,'" Lila's voice went up in imitation of her co-worker. "What about yours?"

"Oh, after Kelli calmed down, it was fine. The interns were nosey, but they tried to be inconspicuous. The board of my company is ecstatic. Great press."

"Nothing from your sister?"

"A few texts warning me to take it slow, but she's known you longer than I have," she laughed. "Jules knows everything, has since day one, so that's about it for people's opinions that I actually care about."

Lila nodded, happy that it at least seemed those who mattered accepted their relationship.

"Things will settle down," Kate said. "I promise. Maybe, we should get away for the weekend? Does that sound nice?"

"It does! Somewhere preferably with no cell service, my mother is driving me insane."

"So you've spoken to her?"

"Briefly, just long enough to confirm that we are in fact together, but she's left a million voice mails and suddenly knows how to text." She didn't know if she should mention getting sick at lunch. She felt much better, and it had only been that one bout of illness, but she still felt off. "I had to cut it short, not that I wanted it to be drawn out. I didn't feel very good; my stomach is still a bit off."

"Are you alright?" Kate turned, giving Lila a thorough looking over.

"I'm fine," she tried to calm her, not thinking it was anything to be overly concerned over, "just nerves, I think."

"If you think you're coming down with something, maybe we shouldn't go."

"I've always had a hair trigger stomach," she lamented, "something you'll have to get used to, I guess."

Kate's look was one of doubt. She wanted to make sure Lila was ok, but she also desperately wanted her all to herself for a few days. "If you're sure."

"I'm sure!" Lila couldn't think of any illness that a few days alone with Kate wouldn't solve.

"Not the Hamptons, though!"

Lila laughed. "Oh, of course, not the Hamptons!"

"You're teasing me."

She slipped her arms around Kate. "Also something you're going to have to get used to, I'm afraid."

"Well, I suppose I can come to terms with it. But seriously, I can't stand all of that, well, that," she said, knowing that from Lila's own upbringing, and especially her mother, Lila knew exactly what she meant. She didn't want to have to dress up for dinner. She didn't want to have hours of inane conversations with people she wasn't overly fond of just because that was what one did; she just wanted to be Kate, off with her girlfriend Lila, not the famous artist, Kate Manderly.

"I want to go somewhere where no one knows who the hell we are." Her phone too had been going off non-stop, to the point where she'd finally turned it to do not disturb and let Jenna filter any important business through to her.

Lila looked unconvinced; pictures of them were splashed across social media. Even if things calmed down quickly, they'd still be noticed in the circles Kate was used to running in.

"Don't worry," Kate smiled, "I know a place."

# 19

The night of the art opening came, and Lila could tell Kate wasn't looking forward to it. She stood in Kate's brightly lit bathroom, watching her glare at her reflection as she put the finishing touches on her makeup. "Have I done something?" Lila ventured, praying she hadn't.

Kate put her eye liner down, turned, stared at her for a long minute, not knowing if she should even broach the subject, not knowing how to even. It frankly, was something she was embarrassed about; embarrassed that she let it bother her, but it still did.

"No," she said, but her morose tone couldn't be overlooked.

"Are you nervous about being in public with me? I promise, I know how to behave and which fork to use," she teased.

"I know that," she took a deep breath, willing herself to speak. "It's the age thing," Lila opened her mouth to speak but Kate held up a hand and she waited. "I know it shouldn't bother me, and when it's just us, it doesn't, but there's no way around it out there in the wild."

Lila knelt before her, taking Kate's hands in hers. "It's wearing on you, I know it is," Lila lamented, "please, don't let it, or at least talk to me about how you're feeling before you let it get to this point in the future."

"I don't think that would be very English of me," Kate said, her voice thick with emotion.

"In that case, you haven't been very English with me yet; you've been you. And, I hate to break it to you, but you're hardly an English ice queen; pretty obvious how you feel about me." That brought a brief smile to Kate's lips. "You can't hide who you are from me," Lila continued, "anymore than I can help being a sappy, love-struck idiot around you, and I am a damn ice queen."

Kate heard what her girlfriend was saying, but still, she couldn't quite shake the feeling she was about to be the subject of tabloid gossip. "I don't like feeling like a fool in public. I don't want to feel like this ridiculous middle-aged woman with her mid life crisis girlfriend, is what I mean."

"I'm not sure whether I should be offended or take me being your 'midlife crisis girlfriend' as a compliment."

Kate sunk into herself, covering her face, "You know I don't actually mean that, in a bad way."

Lila sighed, stood and wrapped her arms around Kate's shoulders. "I know that, and so will everyone else, eventually. I'm in this for the long haul, I swear."

Kate reached out and rifled her fingers through Lila's hair. "I know that, I really do," she breathed. "I took such a hit with Wes, so very publicly. It hurt my pride. Especially seeing him with those younger women, like I wasn't enough anymore."

Lila understood that Kate saying she'd taken a 'hit' with Wes was putting it mildly, more like she'd been run over by a freight train. She hoped that once they were publicly out as a couple, beyond that first morning photo op, they wouldn't be news anymore. They could just be themselves again, together, accepted for having the amazing connection they did. She slapped Kate's thigh. "Finish getting ready woman, or we'll be beyond fashionably late."

Kate's eyes narrowed at the teasing tone of Lila's voice, but her lips turned up, amused. "I need a kiss first, for luck."

Lila didn't need a reason to agree; she was always more than happy to press a kiss to her girlfriend's soft lips. Her hand slid up the nape of Kate's neck as she placed a delicate kiss on her lips. "You don't need luck, but there you go."

———

Everyone in the small coterie of press wanted a picture of the new couple, and despite Kate's protests that she wanted them to focus on her former student's show, it was clear that she and Lila were the evening's major draw. Cameras clicked away the second the couple stepped from the car; Lila was getting a good dose of just what it meant to be in public with Kate Manderly. Every time she heard someone shout her name, she kept assuming it was someone she knew, only to find that as soon as she turned towards the voice, a photographer's flash went off.

She sighed as they finally made their way into the crowded gallery; it was going to take some getting used to, but, as she felt Kate give her hand a squeeze, as their eyes met and Kate gave her that smile that warmed her right through, she knew it was all going to be worth it.

It was mesmerizing to watch Kate work a room, Lila thought, wondering how anyone could ever have a cross word to say about a woman that came off so genuinely warm and sincere. Kate knew everyone's name, something Lila was notoriously terrible at, remembered where everyone worked, who they were with. Probably knew their favorite color, Lila mused, as she was introduced to each.

"Devon!" Kate called, arms wide for an embrace as a handsome young man swooped in. Lila recognized the name, knowing he was the artist whose show they were at. She had the briefest flash of jealousy before she realized that Kate's flirtatious nature was indeed a force unto itself, just as Imogen warned her. It couldn't be turned off. But, just as quickly as her jealousy flared, it vanished as she felt Kate's hand graze her leather clad hip, drifting casually, but purposefully over her backside, pulling her tight to her side.

"My god," Devon grinned at Lila, his grey eyes twinkling, "you are gorgeous!" He gave her hand a friendly squeeze, then hugged the couple together as Kate laughed. "Well done, Ms. Manderly!" He gave them an approving nod before disappearing back into the crowd.

Lila took a breath, laughed. "Well, I guess I can relax now that I've passed the Devon test."

Kate's eyes were full of mirth. "He can be overwhelming."

"Overwhelming? He's the boy version of you. I'm sure everyone in this room right now is half in love with him. Surely the two of you can't be in the same room without some kind of pheromone overload."

Kate looked back into the throng of artists and buyers, all gushing over the young artist, glimpsed fleetly, arm wrapped casually around an equally beautiful hipster's waist, whom she knew for a fact was not his longtime partner. She looked back at Lila, who had a "told you so," smirk on her face. "Alright! Alright!" she said, nudging her, a dazzling smile lighting her features, drawing several glances from admirers. "Guilty as charged!" She bent her head to whisper to Lila. "Just remember, I'm all yours, love."

———

"Well," Kate smiled, "I think that came off well," she said, flicking on her apartment's lights and stepping out of her heels.

"You sound surprised."

"I don't know exactly what I thought the first time showing up with you on my arm would be like, but I didn't expect everyone to be so happy for us."

"It was nice," Lila said. "I didn't want to tell you before, but I was totally freaked out. I know I've been to a hundred art openings but, obviously, this one was different."

"I can't tell you the last time I had any fun at one, except for tonight." Kate was beaming, her thumb brushing over the apple of Lila's cheek. "I think I could be happy doing almost anything so long as you were there."

"And no one made any cracks about a midlife crisis?"

"None that I heard at least."

"Good, now, take me to bed."

———

They were a success, and Kelli called in the morning to congratulate them. It would seem that Lila Croft and Kate Manderly were the celebrity couple of the moment, and the two of them were all too ready to leave it all behind for what they hoped would be a quiet sojourn.

"This isn't a place, it's an airport!" Lila said as they pulled up to the private airfield Friday evening.

Kate feigned innocence. "Are you telling me an airport isn't a place?"

She shot Kate a look. "You know what I mean." Their car pulled onto the jetway, right to the steps of a waiting plane; Kate's plane.

"I do, but I wanted to take you some place special. I know you don't want me trying to sweep you off your feet with all the bells and whistles that come with being with me, but let me spoil you a little."

Lila sighed. It was true; she wanted Kate to feel absolutely secure because she wasn't with her for the money or the perks, but even she had to admit, it was nice having a partner with the ability to jet off at any given moment.

"It'd be a tad ridiculous, I guess, for me to be mad at you for whisking me off on an adventure."

"Oh," Kate grinned, "no adventure here! Just you, me, a bed, and an amazing view."

Lila shook her head, but she was smiling as they boarded the jet. "Next you're going to say something like, 'The view where we're going isn't half bad either.'"

Kate looked slightly abashed. "I absolutely would have said nothing that cheesy. I might have been thinking it," she winked, "but I certainly would not have said it." She pulled Lila down the aisle to two plush leather seats facing each other, sighing with relief as she sat, "Let's do this."

"Ms. Manderly," a pilot stepped out of the cockpit, greeted them, "Ms. Croft," he said, tipping his head in Lila's direction, "flight time this evening is going to be six hours and twenty-four minutes, give or take." A flight attendant joined him, "This is Beth, anything you need, please let her know."

"Thank you, Peter," Kate said to the pilot, dismissing him before turning her brilliant smile onto the blushing flight attendant. "Beth, pleasure to meet you, two glasses of champagne, if you please," she smiled again at the flight attendant, who grinned back and quickly left them.

"Should I be jealous?" Lila asked, eyes following the tight skirt of the leggy blonde.

"I hope you aren't serious."

Lila turned to Kate with a wink and a grin. "A six-hour plane ride? Where are we going?"

Kate looked supremely pleased with herself. "It's a surprise. Don't worry, I'll have you back in time for work Monday; there's a bed in the back. We can sleep, or not, on the way home."

"I don't even have my passport! Which I assume I'm going to need if the flight is that long!"

"I may have nicked it last time I was over."

"You stole my passport?"

"It was just sitting there in your bedside drawer. I saw it the other night, and it gave me an idea. Please don't be mad at me."

Lila's eyes narrowed, but her tone was light. "So long as you promise lots of sex somewhere private."

"Very private, I swear!"

"You're insane!"

"But in a good way, right?"

"The best way!"

Kate's eyes were full of mirth as she smiled back at Lila. "After we take off, I want you back in that bed."

Lila blushed as she took a sip of the champagne; Kate would get no complaints on that request from her.

———

"I have to admit, I've never fucked on a plane," Lila said as Kate led her to the back cabin.

Kate didn't care to respond to the inferred question; of course she and Wes had been together on the plane, in the same bed, many times before. She was going to have to get a new plane, she realized, cringing at the thought of Wes in bed with her. If she dwelled on the thought any longer, she realized, she'd go down the rabbit hole of self loathing and repulsion at her ex.

Instead, her brows lifted suggestively as she pushed Lila back down on the bed, mounting her, her hands grasping at Lila's slim hips. Her teeth clenched in need and anticipation as her chest tightened.

"Prepare to be fucked on a plane then," her smile was almost predatory and Lila's heart thundered in her ears; there was nothing in this world like Kate Manderly when she was aroused like this; when she was like some primal sex goddess about to worship in the only language worth knowing. She swallowed hard; Kate's hands bordering on rough as they edged under her t-shirt, pulled her delicate lace bra down, exposing her small but round breasts, nipples hard and pink, not even bothering to take it off as she bent her head to suck viciously at one, then pulling the other into her mouth, her tongue rough against the sensitive buds.

Kate's thighs were splayed wide, her jean clad pelvis thrusting against hers. Her hands moved to find purchase on Kate's ass as she heard her own groans and gasps mounting; Kate's hair covering her, her tongue swirling lower now, sliding over her taut stomach, teasing at her belly button, causing her to buck as it made its way over the sensitive flesh below her hip bone.

Lila ground her teeth against the screams held just behind them; the release she wasn't ready for. Her head thrashed, and she had a fleeting moment of realizing her hair was destroyed, then not giving a damn as Kate's teeth nipped at her waistband. She felt the button of her jeans give way and then the welcome sound of her zipper, the cool air of the plane's cabin meeting her exposed flesh. Every bit of her was electrified as Kate's naked body met hers, both knowing release would come all too quickly.

———

The pilot's voice roused Lila from her sleep. "Ladies?"

She lifted her head, trying to adjust her eyes from the pitch black cabin to where the pilot stood, a dark silhouette against the light of the main fuselage. "Hmm?" She murmured in acknowledgement.

"We'll be touching down in Inverness in about twenty minutes," he said and turned, leaving Lila with a still softly snoring Kate draped over her. She nudged the sleeping form of her girlfriend, getting no response other than an adorable snort and groan as Kate burrowed deeper into her side. Lila smiled and stroked at the tangled curls tickling her cheek. "Kate? Kate?"

Kate's eyes fluttered as she tried to get her bearings. There was a loud whirring noise all around; she was in her plane, Lila was beneath her. *Right,* she thought, *got it.* Her mouth was dry and the jet's engines were doing nothing for the slight headache that always seemed to accompany long flights. She rolled, leaving the preferred warmth of Lila's body, turning on the compartment's lights, wishing she hadn't.

"God, do you have any water over there?" she croaked at her girlfriend.

She shot Kate a look. "We're in Scotland?" Lila was incredulous. She knew they had to be going somewhere far, obviously for the plane ride to be as long as it was, but Scotland seemed more off the beaten path to her than she'd expected.

Lila grunted as Kate climbed over her, ignoring the question in her quest for water.

Lila watched in silence as she guzzled down a bottle, wiped her mouth, and sighed.

"Done?"

"Yep."

"Yep? You just know a place, in Scotland?" She slid from the bed, maneuvering in the tight space, tugging her jeans up over her hips, shrugging her shirt and a heavy sweater over her head. "How many houses do you have?"

Kate's ass was taunting her as she was peeking out the window into the brightening dawn of the impending Scottish morning. "It was my grandmother's, alright?" she said, rummaging on the ground for her own clothes, "I told you she was Scottish." She sat on the bed, pulling her rain boots over her jeans.

Lila glanced over at the thick rubber boots. "Should have known by the shoes. Thank god you told me what to pack!"

"You said private!" Kate shrugged into a cashmere cardigan, pulled a beanie out of her carry-on and squashed it on over her head, ringlets escaping at will. "Nothing is more private than my Gran's cottage. Just you, me, a caretaker down the road, and some cows."

"She left it to you and Imogen?"

"She did, but Imogen hates Scotland, thinks it's too cold and wild. I love it, so she sold me her half a few years back. I hardly ever get to come here. Maybe that can change now, if you like it of course."

Lila softened, touched Kate would want to share something special with her so soon. "I can't see how I could hate anything that's special to you."

"Rainy and cold isn't everyone's cup of tea."

"You're my cup of tea so I'll love it no matter what."

"Did you seriously just say that?"

"Yes, please don't tell anyone, ever," Lila blushed.

"I make no promises," Kate grinned back, "just know I have that hanging over your head for the rest of our lives."

"So long as we're together."

"Careful, your sweetness is showing again."

"Bitch," Lila laughed, knowing they were in private but honestly, not giving a damn if anyone saw her being head over heels in love with Kate.

———

The weather, when the plane's door opened, was every bit what Lila would have thought of as typical Scottish weather. Even though, back in New York, it was early Fall, where the weather could be anywhere from ninety to forty, as she stepped into the Scottish morning, she was hit with a blast of icy, damp air; pelting, almost frozen drops of rain stinging against her skin.

She pulled her scarf up over her mouth and nose, thankful she'd worn one; she was always freezing on planes and reflexively pulled her hand back as it touched the slick handrail of the plane's steps.

"I'm starving!" Lila groaned into the frosty air as her stomach rumbled. Men were carrying their scant luggage to a waiting Range Rover as they descended the tight stairs; the view of Kate's backside swaying invitingly in front of her, distracting to such a degree that she missed the last step and tumbled into the outstretched hand of the pilot.

"You alright miss?"

"Fine, thank you" she caught her breath and attempted to tidy her disheveled hair as Kate watched, trying not to laugh. She got her hat back on her head and gave Kate a look. "You do that on purpose, don't you?" she asked as she met Kate by the Rover.

"Do what?" she asked, feigning innocence.

Lila shook her head, "That's what I thought," she smiled. "You're dangerous."

Kate's grin was wide, her white teeth shining against the dark morning. She hooked her arm through Lila's and said, "I had coffee and scones left in the car. I can't promise the coffee will be hot, but we still have about an hour's drive and it's certainly better than nothing."

"Damn, this is some life you lead."

"We lead." Kate casually slipped an arm over Lila's shoulder, tucking her close into her side as they reached the car. "I hope you can get used to it."

"I think I'll survive."

Kate's eyebrows raised, and her eyes lit with mirth. "You haven't seen the way I drive yet."

# 20

Kate had called her grandmother's place a cottage, and that was exactly what they came upon an hour later. The Range Rover's tires crunched on the gravel drive as they took the path off the main road. Lila breathed a sigh of relief as the car came to a stop; prying her fingers from the grab handle above the door, thankful they'd arrived in one piece.

"You alive?" Kate teased as she caught sight of Lila's wide eyes. There was a reason she preferred driving alone, after all. Lila swallowed, nodded, thankful they'd been in an SUV instead of a sports car, certain Kate would have put any vehicle she was driving through its paces. It was a harrowing hour of narrow roads and near collisions with a wide variety of roaming wildlife, including a dozen cows, but they were finally there.

Once out of the car, Lila breathed, and stepped back to admire the scene of postcard beauty that was Kate's home. The little structure sat amongst the brown and green of the glen; a loch, silent and still behind it. The low-slung cottage was made of whitewashed stone with bright, sapphire blue shutters, and a blue wooden door. In the dim morning light, Lila caught the glow of firelight coming through the thick lead glass window panes and she felt for all the world as if she were about to enter another realm.

The sound of the car's hatch closing shook her from her reverie; she turned to see Kate pausing a moment to take in the view as well. Somehow she'd still never gotten over the breathtaking majesty of the place.

Kate caught Lila watching her and tossed a small bag in her direction, throwing her own backpack over her shoulder and hefting their other two bags. "Not bad, huh?"

"Understatement." She waited on Kate to unlock the door, but Kate laughed.

"It's open. No one out here but the cows."

———

The cottage was every bit as cozy on the inside as it looked from the outside. It reminded Lila of her family's lake house, the one place where she hadn't felt like an outsider growing up; where her love of fishing and the outdoors could be indulged. Something she'd greatly missed living in cities all her adult life.

Kate's eyes softened, her entire body seeming to relax into the calm of the place as the women entered. The smoke of the little peat fire filled the home with its earthy aroma; she'd phoned ahead and asked the caretaker to get it started when he'd stopped by to open the place that morning.

As promised, there had been lukewarm coffee and delicious scones in the car, neither of which Lila had touched on their winding journey. Kate was starving herself, and knew Lila must be as well. Bless old Ben, she thought, spying the still hot pot of coffee on the brewer and a basket she knew would contain sandwiches and cakes from his sweet wife. They'd known her since she was a girl, running wild as any Bronte character across the moors.

Half an hour later and they were trudging over grass, still wet with morning dew. "You seem different here, you know," Lila said as they ducked under a half fallen post fence. Kate wanted to waste no time in showing the place to Lila, who was finding it stunning. She'd never seen light fall quite the way it did in the Highlands; the strange mix of dark thunderclouds and streaming, golden light; if she ever got the chance, she would have to bring her paints up here.

Kate laughed. "Of course I do, no one's watching," her boots were mud-caked and there were flecks of the stuff over her sweater and speckling her bright hair from the brisk ride they'd taken on her four wheeler to reach the loch.

"I'm watching," Lila said, "so are the cows," she pointed at a particularly shaggy fellow, "that one's been staring you down like he means business," she nudged Kate and winked.

Kate ignored the joke. "Ah, you and I both know that's another thing altogether. I can be at ease here, not feel like I'm anything other than who I am."

"I don't really think there's much difference between you in public and you in private," Lila smiled, "maybe you swear more when we're alone, and now that I think of it, you are oftly cuddly in private."

Kate's elbow dug playfully into Lila's side. "Hush you!" She was smiling, but something about what Lila had said bothered her; she didn't want to be the same person in public as she was in private and instantly felt the sting of a loss. Very few people ever saw her like this; the tomboy, racing about in the mud, traipsing through the moors.

How long was it since she'd ridden her motorcycle or felt the ache and wonderful exhaustion after a full day outdoors? It was no less a part of her than the glamorous, aloof artist, yet, she realized, by keeping this part so private, maybe even she had forgotten it existed. Not that there was a big difference, but being in the public meant there were handlers, PR people, her assistant, drivers, and the list went on; a buffer between herself and reality she could no longer ignore. It couldn't continue if she was to be truly happy; something had to go.

"I never thought I'd be famous. It was never my goal. I thought I'd paint, maybe own a little gallery, marry and have some kids. Fame was never what I was after. You know, all of that, all the fuss and people always around, that isn't who I am; just a necessary evil. I hope you know that."

Lila was slightly taken aback by Kate's sudden change of tone; she sounded offended by what was meant as an offhand remark. Kate continued, "I won't pretend my upbringing wasn't privileged, but I'm certainly not one of those people who can't even make a pot of tea."

"Or slog through muck while carrying heavy objects." Lila nodded her head towards the picnic basket Kate had hefted onto her shoulder.

Kate gave her a look, but didn't speak. They continued walking in silence for a few more moments, hands entwined, Lila's head against Kate's shoulder, before coming to the windswept edge of the loch. Lila helped Kate set the heavy basket down; unpacking a thick plaid blanket, plates, silverware, and the food so kindly provided for them, before the two sat, huddled together in the cool morning.

Kate finally broke the uncomfortable silence. "I always wanted to retire here, putter about the farm, drink whisky, live in sweaters. It's funny though, I never saw myself here with Wes. He hated when it was just the two of us, out here, all isolated. Should have been some kind of warning." Her tone seemed to indicate whatever internal storm had been brewing, passed.

"Well, there's nothing better I can possibly think of than being alone with you," Lila responded.

Kate's eyes narrowed. "Even if it's only just the two of us?"

"I'm pretty sure that's what I said. Maybe we could get a dog? You're not a cat person, are you?"

Kate's lips pursed. "You know what I mean, love."

Lila didn't at first, then she realized; *kids*, the awkward subject she brought up that first afternoon they'd spent together. Lila grasped Kate's arm. "I never meant to bring that up! It's not important to me, I swear! I don't even know if I want kids, it's not something I've honestly given much thought to. I didn't even ever think I'd find someone," she paused, then blundered on, "someone I would want to spend the rest of my life with, but that's what I want with you. Ok? We have plenty of time to figure out what that looks like, don't we?"

"I guess so. I know I sometimes overthink things and make them far more difficult than they need to be. I'm sorry." She shook her head, her curls catching the weak golden light over the hills. "I didn't mean to spoil the moment. I believe you were just saying you wanted to spend the rest of your life with me?" Her face brightened with the question.

Lila couldn't hide her grin. "Something like that."

Kate pulled her close and kissed her. Lila melted into the embrace, the kiss, and couldn't have told a soul what she and Kate had been discussing seconds before. Her entire existence was wrapped up in Kate Manderly's arms.

———

After breakfast, the two slogged back to the cottage, frozen and wet. The little fire was down to a pile of smoking embers. "Let me get this going again," Kate muttered, and then I'll join you in the shower. It's just through there," she waved a hand at an opening. Lila assumed there was a bedroom somewhere. Kate hadn't taken the time earlier for a grand tour, not that there was anything grand about the place.

She followed Kate's non-directions and found herself in a cozy bedroom. There was a double bed, a window looking out onto the moor, a bedside table, a trunk at the foot of the bed, and that was it. That was it aside from the blown out wall, which was now entirely glass. The new space extended another fifteen feet or so, opposite the bed. This was Kate. The floor in the new section was covered by a paint-splattered drop cloth, and a half finished canvas sat propped against the glass wall.

Lila imagined the room must have once been outfitted in floral and lace furnishings as all such places seemed to be. Now though, it was unmistakably Kate's domain. One of her paintings, a black, white, and ochre piece, hung above the bed, taking up most of the wall space. The bed was piled with white linen covers and a thick duvet, a faded ochre velvet throw, complimenting the painting, artfully draped. The window was bare, and the grey mid-morning light looked to be the only means of illumination.

Through another opening, Lila found the bathroom, an apparent modern addition. Lila wasn't complaining. She was freezing. There was a pharmacy cabinet stuffed with fluffy towels, and it took no time at all for the little room to fill with warm steam.

"I thought you'd be naked by now," Kate's voice and hands startled Lila, whose eyes were closed, as she breathed in the calm atmosphere.

She jumped at Kate's voice and the arms winding themselves around her. "God! You scared me!" she laughed.

"Sorry love," she gave Lila a peck on the cheek. "Best get in though, I did what I could with the plumbing in the remodel, but there's still not enough hot water."

Lila did as she was told, grimacing as she pulled her sodden clothes over her head, slid the mud-caked jeans down her legs. "I hope there's a washer in here?"

"It's not quite so primitive," Kate smiled, kicking off her own jeans, leaving her nude, blushing as Lila raked her gaze over her. Kate's lips quirked, taking Lila's hand and leading her into the glass and metal enclosure. The water was hot, too hot, and Lila yelped as it sluiced over her body.

"There we are," Kate said, adjusting the temp, sliding her arms over Lila's shoulders, pressing her body against hers. Lila groaned as their breasts met, their stomachs, their thighs. She could never decide which part of Kate she wanted to get her hands on first.

Kate woke in the night with a start; her body was ice cold. She'd somehow thrown off the warm feather duvet and sheets in her sleep, and now, as she sat up, she saw her breath frosting in the air. "That's not supposed to happen," she whispered.

Lila, being the light sleeper that she was, awoke at Kate's voice. "Shit," she said as, even still snuggled beneath the layers of bedding, she felt the cold air against her face. "Why is it so cold?"

Kate stood, wrapping a soft cashmere blanket around her nude form,

her breath catching as her feet hit the icy wooden floor. "Radiator's on the fritz, looks like," she said as she neared the unit by the bed. "Hold on," she slipped through the moonlit room towards the door.

"Where are you going?" Lila asked.

"I'll be right back," came her voice from the other room. She returned a moment later with a long, heavy-looking wrench.

She crossed the room and gave the radiator a good whack with the tool, a hissing sound escaping as the ancient contraption sputtered back to life. Kate nodded, pleased with her handiwork. Her hair wild and mussed from sleep, the blanket wrapped around her, failing to conceal a shoulder, a moon-blanched breast, with the wrench slung over her shoulder, Lila thought she had seen nothing as sexy in her whole life; Rosie the Riveter as a Celtic goddess.

"That should do it," Kate said, dropping the wrench in the corner before slipping back beneath the covers. Her feet were freezing as they came into contact with Lila's.

"How did you know how to do that?" she asked, impressed and insanely turned on.

"You grow up in old houses, you learn how to fix things, unless you have the patience to wait around for someone else to fix them, and you know I'm not the patient sort. My cousin designed the new additions, but she was still in architecture school, and we never got round to the more mundane upgrades."

Lila gave a little snort of laughter; her love was the antithesis of patient. Still, the thought of little Kate wandering her family's home with a tiny bag of tools brought a smile to her lips. She thought she'd never be done discovering all the facets there were to this wonderous creature beside her, and she was just fine with that. She pressed her warm feet to Kate's frozen ones and snuggled up tight against her. "You're incredible," she sighed, her finger tracing up a warm ribcage. Kate groaned with need, stretching her spine, allowing Lila full access to explore her magnificent body.

By now, there wasn't a blessed inch of Kate that Lila didn't know, but her fascination and ardor remained. Her thumbs brushed over her nipples, her mouth capturing Kate's in a hungry kiss as their hips met; Lila pressing them firmly into the mattress. The hot slickness of their cores meeting again and again; Lila's teeth clenched in a mighty effort to slow herself.

Kate responded to Lila's retreat by raking her nails across her back, "Don't be gentle with me," Kate rasped, "not now!"

It was all the permission Lila needed to lose herself in the moment. She used her fingers to open Kate, splaying her wide, their breasts sliding against each other before she repositioned, pulling a nipple roughly into her mouth, pleased as she heard Kate's corresponding yelp of pleasure.

"Tell me you're mine," Lila gasped, breaking from Kate's swelling breast. Her entire body was writhing in a wanted struggle against Lila's; every

thought obliterated by the rhythmic pulsing of Lila's fingers within her, of her mouth and tongue, stripping every nerve to a single point of pleasure, ready to explode. "I'm yours!" she gasped as her eyes locked with Lila's. "I'm yours! Please, don't stop!" Her last scream of release echoing through the small, dark cottage.

————

Kate woke in the night with a start; her body was ice cold. She'd somehow thrown off the warm feather duvet and sheets in her sleep, and now, as she sat up, she saw her breath frost in the air. "That's not supposed to happen," she whispered.

Lila, being the light sleeper that she was, awoke at Kate's voice. "Shit," she said as, even still snuggled beneath the layers of bedding, she felt the cold air against her face. "Why is it so cold?"

Kate stood, wrapping a soft cashmere blanket around her nude form, her breath catching as her feet hit the icy wooden floor. "Radiator's on the fritz, looks like," she said as she neared the unit by the bed. "Hold on," she slipped through the moonlit room towards the door.

"Where are you going?" Lila asked.

"I'll be right back," came her voice from the other room. She returned a moment later, with a long, heavy looking wrench.

She crossed the room and gave the radiator a good whack with the tool; a hissing sound escaping as the ancient contraption sputtered back to life. Kate nodded, pleased with her handiwork. Her hair wild and mussed from sleep, the blanket wrapped around her, failing to conceal a shoulder, a moon- blanched breast, with the wrench slung over her shoulder, Lila thought she had seen nothing as sexy in her whole life; Rosie the Riveter as Celtic goddess.

"That should do it," Kate said, dropping the wrench in the corner before slipping back beneath the covers. Her feet were freezing as they came into contact with Lila's.

"How did you know how to do that?" she asked, impressed and insanely turned on.

"You grow up in old houses, you learn how to fix things, unless you have the patience to wait around for someone else to fix them, and you know I'm not the patient sort."

Lila gave a little snort of laughter; her love was the antithesis of patient. Still, the thought of little Kate wandering her family's home with a tiny bag of tools brought a smile to her lips. She thought she'd never be done discovering all the facets there were to this amazing creature beside her, and she was just fine with that.

She pressed her warm feet to Kate's frozen ones and snuggled up tight against her. "You're incredible," she sighed, her finger tracing up a warm ribcage. Kate groaned with need, stretching her spine, allowing Lila full access to explore her magnificent body.

By now, there wasn't a blessed inch of Kate that Lila didn't know, but her fascination and ardor remained. Her thumbs brushed over her nipples, her mouth capturing Kate's in a hungry kiss as their hips met; Lila pressing them firmly into the mattress. The hot slickness of their cores meeting again and again; Lila's teeth clenched in a mighty effort to slow herself.

Kate responded to Lila's retreat by raking her nails across her back, "Don't be gentle with me," Kate rasped, "not now!"

It was all the permission Lila needed to lose herself in the moment. She used her fingers to open Kate, splaying her wide, their breasts sliding against each other before she repositioned, pulling a nipple roughly into her mouth; pleased as she heard Kate's corresponding yelp of pleasure.

"Tell me you're mine," Lila gasped, breaking from Kate's swelling breast.

Her entire body was writhing in a wanted struggle against Lila's; every thought obliterated by the rhythmic pulsing of

Lila's fingers within her, of her mouth and tongue, stripping every nerve to a single point of pleasure, ready to explode. "I'm yours!" she gasped as her eyes locked with Lila's. "I'm yours! Please, don't stop!" Her last scream of release echoing through the small, dark cottage.

# 21

Neither Kate nor Lila wanted to be back in the city; it was the first full week of being a couple in public and it was exciting, but stressful. Kate decided a quiet night, alone with Lila at her studio was just what they needed.

After Scotland, Lila seemed more at ease around her, not that she hadn't been comfortable before, but, now, after seeing, what Kate hoped she'd realized was her more chill side, Lila didn't seem to be as affected by the trappings of money and fame that were now a part of her life. Kate wanted her to realize she was still a real and vulnerable person and that she knew how to fix a radiator! She laughed internally. She just wanted Lila to know who she was at her core, and she felt they'd gotten closer to that than ever on their trip.

The table was set; the candles were lit, champagne was chilling in a bucket; she wanted this night to be perfect. After the last few days of turmoil and the jet-lag, they needed this.

No prying eyes, no cameras or questions, just the two of them, as it had been in Scotland.

For years now, Kate's studio had been her refuge. When the "muse was upon her," as she would say, she'd spend days there painting, eating, and sleeping, when she exhausted herself in the white walled converted warehouse. On most days, it was a pleasant place to be; interns running around, asking questions, Kate admitted she rather enjoyed the role of teacher. The best days, though, were when she shooed them all out, and it was just her art and herself. And now, of course, she was welcoming Lila into that bubble.

She was nervous. It excited her that Lila made her nervous, made her care. She hadn't been sure after Wes that she'd be able to care about anyone again, and "care" was a very tame term for what she felt towards her girlfriend.

―――――

There were scallops for the first course, followed by a black truffle risotto and chocolate lava cake for dessert. Kate cooked none of it, but she hoped the sentiment behind the food made up for her lack of domestic goddess skills. And then hopefully, the night would end with them sleeping, well, not sleeping, in the loft where her actual talents could be put to good use. Kate had tidied the little room, which had, in another life, served as the foreman's office, as best she could, but she always thought the artistic messiness of it was part of its charm.

She was tinkering with the lighting, trying to make it romantic as opposed to the forced daylight lighting of work hours, when she heard footsteps downstairs. She went still. It couldn't be Lila. She didn't have a key. Jenna maybe, coming to ensure her boss hadn't burned the place down trying to reheat dinner. Or one of her interns?

She poked her head around the doorframe. And there was her ex-husband, Wes, strolling across the white floor like he owned the place; he never had. She felt heat rise in anger as she stood on the stair's landing, pushing at the escaping locks of her hair as they fell into view.

The sight of him in her sacred space was like a punch to the gut. "Out!" she said, pointing her finger towards the door. "You have no right to be here! Leave the key!" She wasn't screaming, but her tone brooked no questions on how she felt about the man coming towards her. He'd caught her in her disheveled, nervous state, pissing her off all the more as she noted his perfectly tailored three-piece suit and calm demeanor.

He held his arms out, palms up, in a show of compliance. "Hey, I'm not here to fight. I just wanted to see you. I know things have been crazy, and I just wanted to make sure you were alright."

She flew down the stairs, her heavy combat boots clanging on the metal steps. "I don't want to see you! How did you even know I was here?"

"You're always here when you're stressed. When you want to hide. Heard you ran off to Scotland last week too. Things going that bad with your little escapade?"

She pursed her lips in annoyance that he was right, partially right. Like it or not, which she definitely did not, they were together for over twenty years, and there wasn't a thing about her he didn't know. Of course, he would know she was stressed with all the media attention, but damn him for acknowledging it! And damn him for calling what she and Lila were building an 'escapade'!

"I'm fine! Better than fine, not that it's any of your business. So, you've seen me, leave before I call the police."

"I have seen you," he kept walking towards her, a smirk on his handsome face. "I really have, and I want you to know how sorry I am that I didn't earlier. Things never should have gone the way they did." He reached a hand up, fingers ghosting over her hair. His head bent towards her as if he meant to kiss her.

She was tall for a woman, but he was taller still. She felt his breath against her ear. Kate shuddered at their closeness, but couldn't move. "You have paint on your cheek," he said, smiling down at her. He made to wipe the streak of blue away with his thumb, but Kate flinched, stepping back.

"What do you want, Wes?"

He looked her up and down and she realized it made her skin crawl, "You, obviously."

"You cannot be serious!" She stared daggers at him, her mouth agape at the absurdity of his words. "You put me through two years of hell with our divorce! You humiliated me by flaunting your affairs! And have you forgotten the minor detail of you telling me you *never* loved me?"

He bowed his head, as he had always done when he knew he was caught. "I was angry, hurt. I'm so sorry Kat..."

"Don't you dare call me that! You don't get to call me that ever again!" she hurled at him.

"Fine, Kate. I'm so sorry, I was an idiot. I just got so caught up in all of it and things with you were always so, perfect."

"Oh, please," she rolled her eyes, remembering all the biting little remarks about her appearance, her weight, her "commonness" as he had referred to her ability to be an actual person.

"No, I'm serious," he said, reaching for her hand; out of habit or numbness, she let him take it. "I was complacent, and I took you for granted, and if I'm being honest, you're such a good person, it made me hate you more than a little."

When Kate realized where her hand was, she jerked it free and backed away yet again.

"I'm with someone now. Someone who actually cares about me. Someone who likes my fat ass! Who doesn't take pleasure in making me feel small! Someone who doesn't hate me for being a decent human being!"

He scoffed at that. "The grad student?"

"She's not a grad student, she has a bloody job! And a name!"

"Mmm," he shrugged noncommittally. "Really, how do you think that's going to play out? You know people are laughing at you, thinking you're having a breakdown or mid-life crisis or something. She's just after your money."

"You seem to have come through your embarrassment still in one piece, though, I don't think there's anything for me to be ashamed of, whereas you, well..."

"I got caught with two twenty-year-olds, you just have one, not much difference there. You and I both know any one of your interns would be happy to service you, if that's what you need. We could even share."

"Ugh, you are disgusting. I'm not having some fling!"

"Are you telling me you have serious feelings for this girl?"

"If I do, it's no concern of yours! Now please, get the hell out of my studio! And leave the goddamn key!" she yelled this time through clenched teeth.

"Fine." he took the key off his ring and put it in her outstretched hand. "You know she'll never make you happy like I did." He turned and trudged up the other set of stairs, opened the door, "And you know it was your girlfriend that leaked that photo, don't you?" He shot her a snide smile and let the door slam behind him.

Kate's heart dropped to the floor. *The bastard! The absolute bastard! Ugggh!* She hated him! He was lying, of course he was. He had to be, didn't he?

Kate went to the fridge and pulled out a beer, opened it, let the cold liquid slide down her throat. Lila would be here any minute and she needed to pull herself together, but damn it all to hell. There sat the seed Wes had planted.

———

Fifteen minutes later came the knock she'd been expecting. Kate washed her face, tied up her hair. She wished there'd been time to run home now, to at least put on something more date night appropriate, but standard holey, paint-stained jeans and an equally paint splattered t-shirt, it was. She took a second before opening the door; breathing, eyes closed, focusing on what was before her, not behind.

When she opened her eyes, and the door, Lila stood before her; heat rose in her core and her cheeks. A grin tugged at the corners of her mouth as her eyes met those of the enchanting creature before her and she forgot every word Wes said..

"I'm sorry I'm a little late." Lila ducked her head in apology, tucking a silvery lock nervously behind an ear.

Kate didn't want to get into the whole Wes thing at the moment so just said, "No worries." She stepped aside and motioned at Lila. "Come in! I'm sorry this has all been so crazy!" she said, ushering Lila inside the cavernous space.

Lila wasn't exactly sure what she was referring to, but she could tell Kate was flustered. She hoped she wasn't the cause of it.

"Yeah, there were actually paparazzi outside my apartment! So weird, and so random; they just pop up and then disappear." She set her bag down and stared at the massive white room. "This is incredible!"

Two towering canvases were propped against each side of the room, the scaffolding required to work on the uppermost parts of the pieces concealing what lay beneath. Half a dozen smaller unfinished works were strewn about, laying on the floor, propped against a chair or sofa. A long wooden table that had to be at least twelve feet sat in the center of the space, draped with un-stretched canvas, all manner of paints and brushes stored neatly atop it.

Kate laughed as her eyes followed Lila's to the orderly supplies. "Interns," she said, "bless!"

Lila shook her head. "I can't believe this is my girlfriend's studio! I can't believe you're my girlfriend!"

Kate's brow furrowed, even as Lila slid her arms around her. "You're handling everything very well."

"Is that a question or statement?"

"Both, I suppose. I'm just glad, I guess, that you seem ok with the press."

Lila shrugged. "Getting there; obviously, it's still weird. I get that being with you incurs a certain level of attention, and it took me twice as long to get ready this morning. I'm terrified of having my choice of wardrobe picked apart by strangers, but I want to be with you. You're beyond worth it. Everything else is just noise."

Kate cocked a brow. "Perhaps?"

Lila grinned, hooking her thumbs in the belt loops of Kate's jeans, pulling her close. "Perhaps?" Her eyes lit as they met Kate's. "There aren't words for what I feel for you." Tears pricked at her eyes, and she felt the welling of emotion in her throat.

"Are you crying?" Kate was floored, and she felt matching tears at the corner of her own eyes. Not once had anyone ever looked at her like Lila was now. This was love. There was no doubt about it.

Lila smiled as she swiped at the tears. "No!"

Kate grinned back. "I love you." There it was, the small phrase that could change lives, and now it was her turn.

Lila stood, transfixed. She of course, had been stopping herself from blurting out the same words since day one, but it was still so early, so soon. She'd stopped herself before because she hadn't wanted to scare Kate away. Her mouth broke into a wide grin. "I love you too!" She reached for Kate, her hands clasping behind Kate's neck as she stood on her toes, pressing a soft kiss to Kate's lips.

Kate's hand ran up beneath Lila's t-shirt, pressing against her spine, bringing her even closer, her lips crushing against Lila's. She groaned, and Kate found a breath to speak. "Can you wait on dinner?"

"I think I can manage," Lila responded shakily.

Kate snickered, pulled the champagne from the bucket and grasped at Lila's hand. "Let's go."

Lila laughed at the sight of Kate's artist refuge; the Bohemian daybed, the floor pillows, oriental rugs piled on top of each other. "You're such a hippie," she said, pulling Kate with her onto the small bed.

Kate smiled back, making no attempt to dispute the statement. "You can call me anything you like, so long as you take off those clothes." She twisted the metal cage from the champagne and expertly popped the cork from the bottle.

Lila's body reared back from Kate's as she straddled her, pulling her shirt over her head as she went. "You mean like this?" Lila teased.

"God, you're beautiful," Kate mused, champagne running over her hand. "I forgot the glasses."

Lila held her hand out for the fizzing bottle. "Who cares?" she said, taking it from Kate. "Open up."

Kate laughed, but did as she was told, letting Lila pour the bubbling golden liquid into her open mouth. She closed her eyes, let it slide down her throat, savoring the clean sharpness of it. Felt it drip from her mouth, down her throat, under her bra, to her breasts.

"Off," Lila demanded, nodding at Kate's shirt, which she immediately removed. Lila's tongue followed the champagne's path over Kate's flesh. Her body shivered under Lila's ministrations, her nipples hard, her jeans wet; dizzy as Lila took the lead in pressing kisses into her damp flesh.

Lila tugged at the loops of Kate's jeans, "You're going to have to lose these too." Lila's breathing was faster now as her body slid against Kate's, both women's loathe to part even to further undress.

"You too," Kate managed, and Lila groaned, standing to shrug out of the rest of her clothes as Kate followed suit.

———

Lila fell asleep curled against Kate, but Kate remained awake; as she'd tried to drift off, content in the warmth of Lila's weight against her, Wes' taunt crept back in and, try as she might, she couldn't help but wonder if Lila had been the one behind their hurried outing. Did it even matter to her if she had been responsible for the leaked photo? They were happy. Things were nearly perfect. She wanted to trust Lila completely, but trust was earned and so far, she'd given it blindly. Maybe she shouldn't have.

# 22

Life seemed good; it seemed settled in the best meaning of the term. Of course, Kate knew what a life spent with someone meant, she'd been married for twenty years after all. She knew some days Lila would drive her crazy, some days Lila would want to throttle her, but the one thing she wanted to think she really believed in was that they loved each other.

For a whole blessed week, it was quiet; domesticity was a welcome escape for them both. Lila slept every night at Kate's place. They both went off to work in the morning, Kate rather later than Lila, but at least she returned to being a functioning human. She was steadily falling back in love with maybe not her work, but at least art itself.

They chanced a double date with Jules and her husband that went well. Jules absolutely adored Lila and was already planning their wedding. Kate told her friend she had no intention of rushing things, though, she was already secretly planning to ask Lila to move in with her.

Lila was snuggled up in Kate's arms, the two having their coffee on the sofa one morning, while Jenna sorted through mail and made a list of the day's to do's.

They heard Jenna gasp. "Oh my god!"

Kate cocked her head back over her shoulder towards the kitchen where Jenna's exclamation came from. "Everything alright?" she called.

Jenna walked in, her face a mask of warring emotions. "Something's come out, in the press."

Kate rolled her eyes. "Ok? What is it? I'm assuming it has something to do with either me, or that boy band you are obsessed with."

"Kate, it's serious," she almost whispered.

Kate motioned at Lila. "Let me up, love," she said, patting her knee.

Lila turned to look back at Jenna as she moved to the other side of the sofa; Jenna didn't meet her gaze. "Kate?" Lila said, as Kate stood and went to Jenna, who was holding out her phone to her boss.

Lila saw the blood drain from Kate's face and was immediately on her feet and moving her way.

Kate whirled on Lila. "What have you done?"

"Kate! What is it?" She knew Kate suspected she had been the one to leak that first photo of them to the press; Kate never said it, and Lila never brought it up, but still anytime that photo of them with their hands on each other outside the restaurant popped up, Kate looked at her in a way that made

Lila feel like she'd done something wrong, even though she hadn't.

Kate didn't speak; Jenna gingerly took the phone from Kate's hand and showed it to Lila. It was the cover of an old newspaper. "Heiress Drowns Self On Holiday," it read in large black print, and below it, there was a photograph of Cecile in apparent happier times, laughing, her black hair piled up on her head, and behind her, just visible in the corner of the frame, was a teenaged Kate.

Lila looked from the screen to Kate, to Jenna. "I don't understand." There were tears coming now; Kate couldn't possibly think she would tell anyone about Cecile, did she?

The new article went on to detail a love affair between Kate and Cecile. The implication was that Kate was the cause of the young woman's death. And there, next to the picture of Cecile, was a picture of herself, smiling, an arm around Kate's waist.

Kate still wouldn't, or couldn't, speak. Jenna spoke instead. "It's intimating that you aren't Kate's first female lover, and that she was the reason this, Cecile, killed herself." It was clear to Lila, even through the fog of panic, that Jenna hadn't known the story about the woman in the painting before now.

"Kate, I swear I didn't do this! Why would I? How can you think I would ever betray you or your trust?"

"You knew about this?" Jenna asked, shocked, but Kate interrupted.

"Because I don't really know you, do I?" Wes' words came back to her; it was Lila that leaked the photo of the two of them to the press. If it was true, Lila forced the issue of making their relationship public. The thought lingered in the back of her mind since Wes said it. She hadn't wanted to believe it then, but now she didn't know what to think.

Kate's accusation crushed Lila; yes, they'd only been together for a few weeks, but they had been the most perfect weeks of her life. It hadn't been easy; it hadn't been stress free, but Kate was worth it; what they had was worth it.

"Kate, I have nothing to gain from this. Please, believe me." The tears were falling now in earnest.

Lila reached for her, but Kate shook her off. "Don't touch me! Don't come near me again."

"You can't mean that," Lila whispered.

"I do." Her mind was racing and all she could see was red. She felt the heat of her anger flash up her cheeks. "This was a farce from the beginning."

"Kate!" Jenna blurted, shocked that Kate could think Lila would do something like this. Of course, she had been wary of the other woman at first, but she'd seen the way they were together, how considerate they were of each other. Kate shot her a look; it wasn't her place to insert herself here.

"Don't do this," Lila said. "I know you've been hurt, but it wasn't me that did it. I think you know that. I think you're scared, and this is just an excuse to push me away."

Kate stopped. Maybe Lila was right. After all, what would she gain from airing her secrets? Still though, this had been a doomed relationship from the start, hadn't it? What could they really have hoped for? If life had taught her anything, it was

Riley West

that happiness couldn't last, so why even look for it? Better that they end it now, before anyone got too hurt.

"You should go," Kate said, squeezing her eyes tight, not wanting to admit to the tears brimming there; admit that it had been too late for her to not get hurt since the moment she first saw Lila at her party. She'd loved her from the start.

"Kate…"

"Now!"

And that was it, Lila thought, her world crashing down before she'd even properly enjoyed it.

———

"You're miserable," Jules said.

"I am not," Kate retorted. It had been two days since she and Lila's blow up, and she was, in fact, miserable.

"Miserable, and petulant. You sound like a petulant teenager. I remember you as a teenager, and this is it all over again. Melodramatic as fuck."

"I was going for apathetic," Kate said, pushing at the salad on her plate, not having the stomach to take a bite. Beyond miserable was an even more apt description of what she was. Lila said that she wasn't the one that gave the story about Cecile's death and her involvement to the media; why hadn't she just believed her? Lila had given Kate no reason not to, but she just couldn't shake this deep-seated distrust.

"Well, you missed. I mean, really, why would you think Lila would have any reason to bring up Cecile to the press?" Her friend asked, needing no explanation as to her current foul mood. "Not when everything was going so well. You two were like gropey newlyweds. Did something happen in Scotland?"

Kate made a face. "Ugh, that bad?"

"That good," Jules said, "things should be like that in the beginning, and you didn't answer my question."

"There's nothing to say; nothing bad happened, it was wonderful! She was wonderful. Is wonderful." Kate dropped her head into her hands, nearly face planting into her eggs benedict. "I just don't know who else would do it, no one has anything to gain from this story coming out, and only a handful of people even knew about Cecile and I."

"Wes does," Jules said. "He clearly wants Lila gone; he said so when he was at your studio."

Kate's eyes went wide as the truth hit her. "Oh god! Jules! How could I have been so stupid?"

"No idea, I told you the same thing days ago. But if he's the one who told you Lila did it, then he's definitely the one actually behind it and probably the Cecile story too."

Her phone was already out, and she was searching through her texts to get to Lila's. "I'm a bloody idiot!" she said, thumb flying over the phone's keyboard.

"Why don't you just call her?"

"I need to see her. This is an apology that has to be made in person. If she'll even see me."

"She should make you grovel; that's what I do to Luke when he's acted like a moron."

Kate glared at her, but jumped up when her phone buzzed; Lila had texted back. "I'm sorry, I have to go, she's just down the street."

———

Lila was at that perfect moment of buzzed uncaring. The world seemed a better place in that state, and even though Kate's angry words were still amongst her thoughts, the cheesy goodness of the queso and the tartness of the margarita in her hand were foremost. It was nice to know that she still had a few good friends left in the city and Liz and her roommate, Christina, who she'd met a handful of times, were now definitely on that list.

The two other women insisted Lila meet them for drinks after work, and, after some prodding, she agreed. She might not think it had been a good idea when she would try to get ready for work in the morning, but for the moment, it was turning out to be a splendid one.

"Are you really not going to at least text her?" Liz was asking, and Lila knew exactly who she was referring to.

Lila didn't want to talk about it, but also desperately wanted to; she needed to at the least get someone else's opinion on the matter, because she was tired of her own internal voice screaming at her to do just that; call Kate.

"You think I should? I didn't do anything wrong! I don't know why she won't trust me!"

"Maybe because the one person she trusted most betrayed her in the worst way possible."

"I already told her that. I told her that I thought she was just scared but she could trust me. I would never hurt her!"

"She'll either get over it or she won't, but I think it's worth having a discussion. You can't leave it with no resolution; super unhealthy," Christina chimed in. "I've been through a lot of therapy," she laughed as the other two women stared at her.

At that moment, Lila felt a sharp pain in her side and looked to see Liz nudging her with her elbow. "Jesus Liz, you have the boniest elbows! What?"

Liz's head nodded towards Lila's phone; the screen was lit and on it was Kate's name and a text. "It's fate," Liz said, a knowing look as she took another sip of her margarita.

"You're going to meet her here?" Liz couldn't believe it; the couple tried very hard to be private, and now Lila was inviting her famous girlfriend to have it out in the very public space of a Mexican restaurant? "I'm not sure that's a good idea. Why don't you go to her place or yours?"

"No." Lila shook her head, self-assured. "I'm tired of trying to hide. Whichever way this goes, it's going to be out in the open so I may as well have some control over it."

"Ok then, Godspeed," Liz saluted.

———

The sky cracked as a loud clap of thunder shook the restaurant and a streak of lightning lit the sky as the friends sat waiting for Kate. "Damn," Christina said, "hope she at least got a cab."

"She didn't." Lila pointed to the large picture frame window and the soaked figure of one Kate Manderly. "Shit," she said, grabbing her umbrella, leaving the table and heading for the door as Kate held up a hand in acknowledgement.

There was a tiny vinyl awning on the front of the building that Kate was trying, and mostly failing, to huddle under. The rain was coming in blowing gusts and the overhang was doing little to keep her already soaked form any drier.

She hung her head as Lila opened the restaurant's door, the smell of warm tortillas and a trill of music following her out into the storm.

"Get under this umbrella!" Lila said as she stepped outside and motioned to Kate.

"I'm already soaked," she said, "doesn't matter, and I won't take long." If the rain hadn't done its part to make the usually publicly glamorous Kate look pathetic, the pained look in her eyes would have been enough. "I don't know what it is in me that won't believe that anyone could love me, that you could love me. But I'm so, so sorry. You do not know how sorry I am that I could have destroyed this before we've even properly begun. You're the best thing that's ever happened to me."

Lila was suddenly sober and as Kate finished speaking, her eyes welling with tears, Lila knew the tongue lashing she'd planned was out the window. Of course, Kate had trust issues after her marriage failed in such a spectacular fashion; after she'd found out her husband betrayed her time and time again. It hurt though, knowing that for even one second Kate doubted her. It hurt, but not nearly as much as did the thought of not being with her.

"It's alright," Lila spoke, taking a step towards her, a tearful smile playing at the corners of her mouth. "Nothing broken that can't be fixed."

An echoing smile flickered on Kate's lips, still not fully trusting that Lila could so easily take her back after she had been such an idiot. "Are you sure?" she asked.

Lila nodded, "Yeah, I think you may be stuck with me."

Kate grabbed Lila's coat and pulled her into a kiss. Their tongues crashed against each other and Lila groaned/laughed as the umbrella slipped from her grip and the rain washed over them. Neither cared.

Kate tasted the tequila on Lila's tongue as she too laughed into the kiss. Her perfectly tousled curls were ruined, she knew. Her mascara was most probably running down her cheeks, but she was kissing a beautiful woman in the rain on a street in New York. Nothing else mattered.

A flash broke the moment, not lightning, but a photographer snapping away, capturing the moment Kate acknowledged to the world that yes, she was, in fact, hopelessly in love with the amazing creature in her arms. Her world, their world, would never be the same.

She breathed, took that breath to slide her fingers into Lila's; an interlocking, steadying embrace. "It'll be ok," she whispered to Lila, pulling away just enough to look into those hazel eyes. "I love you."

# 23

The smell of coffee made its way to Lila's sleeping brain, nudging it to wakefulness; the weight of someone sitting beside her on the bed soon following.

"Good morning," came Kate's purr. Lila smiled up at her as her eyes opened onto the lovely vision of Kate, curls piled on top of her head, holding a mimosa out to her.

"You are a goddess," Lila said, taking the flute and drinking the tart beverage.

Kate took a sip of her own and carded her fingers through Lila's messy hair. "Don't forget it. There's coffee too. But don't get used to it, domestic, I am not."

Lila grinned. "You mean I won't be coming home to you waiting for me with a drink ready and dinner on the table?"

"Only if you don't mind Chinese take out every night."

Lila brushed a curl from Kate's face, tenderly tucking it behind an ear, drinking in the sight of her love. How could life be so good, she wondered?

A knock on the bedroom door frame brought their attention to Jenna's compact figure, expertly averting her eyes. In the few weeks they'd been together, Lila had gotten used to the ever present assistant, who was becoming a fast friend.

Jenna stood before them, face white as a sheet. Kate was immediately on her feet. "Jenna!" She took her assistant by the arm to steady her. "Are you alright?"

"Kate, I've done something that you may feel has been an overstepping of our relationship, but I hope you'll understand that I would have done the same for any friend."

*This sounds very not good,* Kate thought. "I think you best be out with it then." Her voice sounded harsher than she'd meant it to, and she saw the responding fear creep into Jenna's expression.

"After the story came out, about, well, the story," Jenna wasn't usually at a loss for words but she was beyond uncomfortable mentioning her employer's lover's suicide. Cecile was a decidedly no go topic, but one that could no longer be avoided if she were to tell Kate the whole truth. "After it broke," she continued, knowing that Kate understood exactly which story she was referring to, "I hired a private investigator. I didn't believe it could be Lila. I'd never seen you as happy before as you were that morning with her, and I had to prove that she wasn't the one to tell the press about your past."

Far from angry, it touched Kate that Jenna would care so much. "Ok," she said, motioning for her to continue.

167

"Well, of course, it is," Kate replied.

"No, he's been tapping your phone for months." Kate struggled for words and found none.

"What the fuck!" Lila blurted. She knew Kate's ex wanted her out of the picture, but this was next level.

"With the case against him, he's desperate. He knows without your money, he's done for. I guess he hoped he could drive a wedge between you and Lila and that you'd come running back to him."

Kate couldn't believe it, except sadly, she could. Wes had always been a manipulative son of a bitch, but he'd never been an unhinged one, as far as she knew. And that night at the studio, she thought something was off. He seemed desperate.

"He's lost his damn mind, then. I don't care if Lila and I broke up or not, I would never go back to him! I didn't realize until I was with Lila how much damage he'd done to me, to my sense of self, but now that I've been with someone who makes me feel like the best version of myself, even with all the bad stuff, someone who actually takes me into account, I could never be with anyone who didn't value me again."

Lila blushed at Kate's words, at her stating her feelings so boldly.

"But, shouldn't we call the police or something?" Jenna asked.

Kate shrugged; the problem had been dealt with after all; they knew what to look for, and Jenna clearly had someone capable of ensuring it didn't happen again. "They've got him already, Jenna. He's not going to see daylight ever again. It'd only be kicking the hornet's nest at this point."

"You know how he is, though, how he can get away with things! What if he gets off? What if he comes after you?"

She put an arm around the younger woman. "Then he'll slink back off to wherever the fuck he's been for the last two years. He's already tried to come between Lila and I, and thankfully, she took me back. Whatever he may think he is to me, I promise you, he'll never be in my life again."

# 24

Lila was staring intently at the dull, grungy tunic of the god Bacchus; she had been cleaning this part of the painting for two weeks with no end in sight, when an intern smacked her on the arm. "Oh my god!" the intern fangirled. "Why didn't you tell me Kate was coming today! I have to get a selfie with her! Please?"

She looked up to see Kate, clad in an uncharacteristically elegant three piece grey tweed suit, tailored of course, to perfection; black heels accentuating the sophisticated figure she was cutting. "I didn't know she was." Lila put her brush down, stripped the gloves from her hands and ran a nervous hand over her short ponytail, attempting to calm her nerves.

It had been hard enough at work since they'd become an item; she felt like people were always staring, even when they weren't. Now, her girlfriend showed up unexpectedly, looking like a 1930s movie star, and of course, with the museum's director in tow.

It was a tortuous forty-five minutes for Lila who hated being the center of attention, though she had to admit, listening to Kate talk about art was damn sexy. Watching her study a brushstroke here, the unmistakable light of a Renaissance sky there. She was enchanting as always, giving words of encouragement and showing genuine interest, not to mention her own vast knowledge, before finally giving a final nod to the director as he mentioned something about lunch.

"I'll be there in just a moment," Kate shot over her shoulder at the man as she winked at Lila. "You're blushing," she whispered as she finally acknowledged her girlfriend's presence.

"I didn't know you were coming today," Lila responded under her breath.

"I didn't know either, but then Edwin," of course, she was on a first name basis with the museum's director, "asked me to lunch. I'm sure he's after a donation, but I thought it would finally give me a chance to pop in."

"You're not wearing a 'pop in' outfit."

A slow smile spread across Kate's lips. "Just think about getting me out of it later." Lila almost dropped her brush at the thought.

"So," Kate teased, "are you going to show me what's behind the curtain?" She had gestured at a covered rectangular object, which, she was assuming was a painting. It looked to be about 11"x17" and draped in a French Blue velvet covering.

Lila grimaced, two blooms of red appearing on her cheeks as she waved a hand in front of Kate's face. "This is not the painting you're looking for."

Kate laughed, "Nice," she said regarding the reference, Lila being one of the few people in her life as big a closet nerd as she was, "but seriously, it's a lost Vermeer or something, right?"

Lila's eyes darted around the room, clocking the pointed inattention of her co-workers. Every one of them was a fine artist themselves, else they wouldn't have the jobs they did, but, girlfriend or not, no one wanted to be critiqued by a famous artist in front of a room full of their peers. "It may be," she responded, keeping her voice low, "or it may be a Lila Croft original that I can't seem to finish."

Kate stopped, immediately sorry for teasing her. "Can you bring it home?" she asked, noting her girlfriend's discomfort.

Lila relaxed a little; she would not get raked over the coals in front of everyone, but that didn't mean she wasn't still nervous for Kate to look at her piece, even in private.

———

Lila cradled the little package against her body the entire way home, using her sharp elbows against the jostling crowds of the evening rush-hour subway. Her eyes lit as she exited the slick station stairs, seeing the outline of Kate leaning casually against the corner of her building; it was becoming a common and most welcome sight.

"Hey you," Kate beamed as she caught sight of Lila.

"Hey you?" Lila laughed. Kate was still wearing the sleek suit and heels. "In that getup you should be smoking one of those long thin cigarettes and asking for my help to stop an international jewel thief."

"I think I prefer to be the thief in this scenario," she quipped, "looking for an accomplice."

"I would so be your accomplice!"

By the time they made it up the stairs, Kate was regretting her shoe choice and was very grateful to kick them off by the front door.

"Uh, what are you doing?" Lila asked as she saw Kate drop four inches.

Kate cocked her head. "Seriously?"

"I've been stuck at work all day with the image of you in that suit and those heels looking like Lauren Bacall and Rita Hayworth's love child. I will not be denied my naughty fantasy."

Kate's lips pursed as she gave in, stepping back into the heels, trying hard not to break into a grin. She loved the rhythm the two of them had eased into; she could be dominant or submissive, seductress or seduced, or simply a woman in love with another woman who loved her in the same deep way. Their roles were fluid, changing with their moods and desires.

"So, what else did this fantasy involve?"

Lila placed the parcel carefully beside the door, hanging her own jacket and bag on the small coat rack. Her hands went to Kate's small waist, "I want," she said, backing her into the galley kitchen, "to take each and every piece of clothing off you, slowly," Kate was against the cabinets now; Lila was peeling the suit jacket down her arms. "Then I want to fuck you, with those heels on, and nothing else."

A blush crept up Kate's throat and cheeks, but her voice stayed throaty, "Oh, you tease."

Lila thrust a knee between Kate's thighs. "I'm not teasing," she said, unbuttoning the fitted tweed vest. She pressed her body hard against Kate's, catching her lips in a rough kiss. Her gaze was unfocused as Lila broke from the embrace to study her. She reveled in her lover's mussed appearance, the flush of her skin, the quickening of her pulse as her hands slipped inside the crisp white blouse that concealed her lush, perfect breasts.

Lila felt a thrill go through her as her hands met Kate's skin, felt her nipples harden at her touch. "God," Kate moaned. Her head thrown back against the cabinets, her eyes shut tight. "That feels divine."

"I couldn't think about anything else all day. I didn't get any damn work done after I saw you."

"I'm not about to apologize," she grinned as Lila slid her pants down her toned thighs, over the black heels. Lila groaned at the sight before her. Kate's statuesque figure was on full display before her, wet and ready. Her tongue swirled over the golden flesh of a thigh before traveling upwards.

She absentmindedly thought it a shame she hadn't had the forethought to break out her handcuffs. It was enough though to watch Kate's fingers dig into the sides of the countertops, her knuckles going white, as she went to work lapping with her tongue; breaking around her as Lila's fingers finished the work.

After, they'd both fit themselves against each other in the tight shower, laughing as one after another got elbowed or kneed in the small space. Lila was stalling. She couldn't help but be nervous about anyone looking at what she considered to be her finest piece of artwork. And Kate wasn't just anybody, beyond being her girlfriend, she was a world class artist.

Kate gasped. The painting before her was every bit as fine as the painting of Cecile, which hung in her bedroom. "Why didn't you say something?"

"What do you mean?"

"When I said 'nobody paints like this anymore'?"

Lila looked down, awkward. "It's just something I painted, for myself. It's not anything near yours." The moonlit sky hung over a stormy sea, much as it did in Kate's larger piece.

"You're wrong, it's breathtaking," she turned from the painting, taking Lila's hands in hers as tears pricked at the corners of her eyes. "You're breathtaking. We should be planning for your show, not mine."

"You said it yourself, there's no money in painting like this. People just want squiggles and bright colors to match their sofa." She looked suddenly abashed. "No offense."

Kate shrugged, a smile on her lips. "None taken! I sold out, made a hell of a lot of money. I did it so I could get back to this," she gestured at the painting before her, "at least that was the plan."

"Wes?"

"Mmm. He saw the potential, and I ran with it. But, now I'm free of him and anything else I wish to be free of, including a style that no longer interests me."

"I want to be there someday too, just painting because I love it, but I'm not really seeing that happening soon. Restoration isn't exactly an overly lucrative field."

"We should run away together," Kate mused, "just be on our own, having sex, painting, having more sex."

Lila groaned, "You do not know how tempting that is." And for the first time, she meant it. She was finally feeling secure enough in their relationship to give the idea actual thought. They could go off and just be together, doing whatever they wanted; they had that ability. Well, Kate did. But going off like that meant leaving her job and a career that she'd finally made headway in. Still, she would be with Kate. If they were both satisfied and secure with that kind of lifestyle, why not?

"Wouldn't it bother you, supporting me like that?"

"One, I'm giving a genuine artist the ability to create and freely express themselves; you wouldn't be the first grant I've handed out. Two, you inspire me. And three, I plan on making a good return on my investment," she grinned, "one way or another. Will you think about it?"

Lila's hands were tangled in Kate's hair, her green eyes wide and soft as they regarded her. "How am I supposed to say no to you?" Lila whispered. *You're my soul*, she thought.

"Table the discussion until after dinner?" Kate said.

"Shit!" Lila turned Kate loose; she'd forgotten they were having dinner with Jules and Luke that night. "I totally forgot!"

"It's ok, I know you were helpless against the power of the suit," she laughed, "But we need to hurry up and make ourselves presentable if we're going to get there on time."

# 25

Kate watched Lila turn green as Jules set the plate of fish in front of her. "Love? Are you feeling alright?"

Lila swallowed hard, feeling hot and queasy; it had been weeks of these nausea waves that she couldn't seem to shake. A cold, snaking suspicion wound its way through her brain over the last few days; one she didn't want to believe, but one that was becoming harder and harder to ignore.

She took a sip of ice water, holding back the bile, and smiled at Kate. "Fine, I just think maybe I better head out."

Kate's brows furrowed. "Are you still not feeling well?" she whispered as Jules and Luke continued bringing in food from the kitchen.

Lila caught another whiff of a passing plate of fish, and nearly lost it right there at the table. "I have to go!"

She stood quickly and nearly collided with Jules, who took one look at Lila and said, "Bathroom's this way!" She grabbed her hand and led her down a short hall, Kate following close behind.

Jules excused herself without a word as Kate moved in to help Lila. She held her hair back as Lila retched into the toilet. "You're going to the doctor tomorrow," Kate said.

Lila nodded weakly, trying not to cry. Trying not to think this might be her last night with Kate.

———

"I'm so sorry about the dinner," Kate said later over the phone to Jules; they'd left as discreetly as possible after Lila had been sick and were now back at her place. Lila was dozing on the sofa, a cold compress on her head.

"Hey," Jules said, "I have four kids. A little puke isn't going to phase me at this point. Is Lila ok though?"

"Yeah, I think so. She can't seem to shake this bug; she's had it since Scotland."

"Too much Haggis?" Jules joked, but really was worried about her best friend's girlfriend. As she'd said, she had four kids and all her pregnancies had come with a good dose of so-called morning sickness and she felt like she knew it when she saw it at this point. But, as Luke pointed out, the only people who really knew what was going on in a relationship were the two people in it, and maybe the supposed pregnancy was something Lila and Kate were keeping secret, or maybe, Lila

179

herself hadn't even realized it yet; either way, it wasn't for her to bring up.

"No such thing as too much Haggis," Kate responded, and though her tone was trying for light, Jules could hear the concern for her partner in her friend's voice. "We'll see you for the benefit tomorrow night? If Lila's alright, of course."

Jules laughed. She loved her kids and being a mom, but there was no way she was going to miss a night out at a swanky party with her husband. "We'll be there! And so will you! It's a big deal, being recognized like this," she said, referring to the humanitarian award Kate was receiving at the party.

"I'm just worried about her."

"Everything will be fine," Jules said, and hoped it was true.

———

Lila ended the call even as the nurse on the other end was still speaking; something about scheduling her next appointment, an ultrasound. She was pregnant. She nearly dropped the phone as she felt the blood drain from her. She had to sit; had to think, figure things out. Figure out what to tell Kate. Her heart dropped; what to tell Phillip? It was his baby. She'd thankfully never found herself in this situation before, but here she was. She knew everything was too good to be true, that life had finally been going right for her. Now this.

Lila needed to tell Kate. She shook her head, trying to regain some wits before making the call, but stopped before she pushed 'dial'. Tell Kate what, exactly? She had no idea what she was going to do, if she'd even keep it, if she'd tell Phillip, what she'd tell Phillip if she did? She felt sick and rushed to the bathroom. All Lila wanted was Kate's arms around her telling her everything was going to be alright, but now, she didn't know if things were ever going to be right again.

Her phone rang; it was Kate. Numbly, she picked up.

"Darling, where are you? Did everything go alright at the doctor's?" Lila nearly burst into tears at her girlfriend's casual tone. But of course, why shouldn't it be casual? Kate had no idea that their world had just come crashing down, and that Lila was to blame. "Darling?"

Lila breathed, shook her head, steeled herself to sound as normal as possible; now wasn't the time for the conversation that was going to have to come.

"I'm here. Sorry."

"Is everything ok?"

"Yeah, it's fine. I was just over at my place. I needed to pick up my shoes for tonight."

"What did the doctor say? Are you sure you're ok to go tonight?"

"I'll be fine tonight, I promise."

"Alright love, I guess I'll see you when you get here." Kate didn't sound convinced.

"I'll be heading out in a minute. Promise I won't be late for my big red carpet debut!"

"You better not be," Kate quipped, and Lila's stomach turned over at what felt like her betrayal.

"Ok, bye," she said. She hung up and promptly threw up. She had to make it through the night, just make it through until she could figure it all out.

# 26

Lila arrived back at Kate's place an hour later. She knew she had to talk to her about the pregnancy, didn't know how she was going to make it through the party without telling her, but as Kate came into view, a crew of hair and makeup artists surrounding her, Lila knew the discussion would have to wait.

"Love," Kate said, noting Lila's pallor as she entered the bedroom, and shooing the makeup artist away, "are you sure you're alright? You look ill. Honestly, I don't think we should go."

The makeup artist, a young woman in her twenties, gave Lila a once over. "Nothing we can't fix." She turned her attention back to Kate and gave her a reassuring smile before going back to the job at hand.

"I'm fine," Lila said, trying to sound light and normal. "You're getting an award for being an amazing human. I'm not missing that and you most certainly are not!" Kate's eyes narrowed; Lila could see she knew something was up, but Kate took a deep breath and nodded for the makeup artist to continue. Whatever Kate thought was amiss could wait, and Lila was all too happy to let that be the case.

————

Lila's jaw dropped as Kate stepped from the bedroom; she'd seen her dressed up before, but never to the A-list celebrity level that she was now. The kelly green v-neck dress was cut to show every one of her assets off to its best advantage; her toned arms and shoulders were bare, the lush curves of her breasts and hips hugged by the fabric before it flared softly around her glittering heels.

She knew she looked good. "Not bad, eh?" Kate raised a brow as she shook her mane of copper curls back over the sweep of her shoulders.

Lila was struggling with her words. She was blown away. "Um, yeah, something like that," she said, turning nervously to study herself in the entry mirror. "Do I pass?"

Her silver dress sparkled in the mirror, her lavender hair styled in shoulder length soft waves, her makeup subtle but perfect.

Kate shook her head and blinked at the tears in them. "You're the most beautiful thing I've ever seen," she said, and meant it. She took Lila's hands in hers. "I hope you really know how much I love you."

Lila wanted to blurt out the truth about her pregnancy, that she was sorry, that she would do anything to stay with her;

instead, she smiled back, holding back her own tears. "I love you too."

————

It wasn't a large event, one just like it took place almost any night in New York, but this one had enough big names in attendance to draw a few members of the always hungry celebrity press.

Lila took a deep breath as the limo pulled to the curb.

"Wes is coming," Kate warned Lila as, moments later, she spotted her ex. Kate's eyes darted around, searching for Jenna or security as Wes came towards them. She didn't want to make a scene; she was tired of being in any way associated with the man.

Lila's stomach dropped; there was nothing good that could come from an encounter with Kate's ex.

"What are you doing here, Wes?" Kate was keeping her voice low, her expression neutral, trying not to draw the unwanted attention of the photographers.

He turned his attention to Lila, looked her up and down and smirked. "Don't you look lovely, Ms. Croft."

"Wes!" Kate exclaimed, stepping between Lila and him. "Please, this isn't the place for whatever this is."

"I bought a ticket for charity, just like everyone else here. My lawyers thought it'd be a good idea, you know, show that I give back and all that bullshit."

*Where the hell is Jenna?* Lila was panicking as she saw people taking note of their huddle.

"You're completely full of shit, Wes, and everyone else knows it now. Why not try to go out with a little dignity?" Kate shot back. Things were getting heated now, their voices louder.

Lila placed a hand on Kate's back. "Maybe take it inside at least?" she whispered, nodding her head towards the growing crowd of onlookers.

Wes' eyes went wide, his falsely charming smile turning into a snarl. "Fuck you, you little cunt! You stand there acting like you haven't been lying to her from day one? She doesn't love you, she's just doing this to get back at me, and when she's done with you, she'll be right back with me!"

"What are you talking about? I love Kate!" Lila flung back at Wes. "I'd never betray her!"

Wes smirked. "Oh really?"

Kate grabbed at his arm, trying to pull him away from Lila. "Wes, you're making a fool of yourself," she angrily whispered, noting the paparazzi clicking away at the scene.

Wes jerked his arm from Kate's grasp. "I'm making a fool of myself?" He turned from Kate back to Lila. "When are you going to tell her you're pregnant?"

Lila's eyes went wide as her heart faltered; her eyes met Kate's stunned gaze; she couldn't speak. Instead, she reached for her, but Kate reflexively flinched.

"Back the fuck off Wes." it was Jenna, who had thankfully been summoned by someone. "Damage done, ok."

"Kate?" Lila spoke through the lump in her throat.

Kate's eyes were glassed over with unshed tears. A million thoughts were running through her head at the moment; she wanted to be anywhere but where she was; somewhere where she could at least hear herself think. Presently, all she heard were the mechanical clicks of cameras and shouts of paparazzi to "look over here".

Jenna's arm went around her waist. "I've got you," Kate nodded, "we'll go in the front and out the back, ok?" Kate nodded again. "Lila?" Jenna asked, almost as an afterthought. She turned to see her standing, looking lost, panic clear in her eyes.

Jenna rolled her eyes, took a deep breath. It wasn't as if she hadn't been smoothing over disastrous public outings between Kate and Wes for years. The last year of their marriage had been tabloid fodder, not to mention the two years it took for their divorce to be final. She gestured at a security guard and he took his cue, stepping between Wes and Lila. "Lila!" Jenna whispered as loudly as she dared, "Let's go!"

The limo door shut behind them, and aside from Jenna, they were blessedly alone.

"Kate," Lila wanted to reach for her hand but stopped herself, not wanting the rejection, "please, look at me."

Kate sniffled, blinked back tears, straightened in her seat. She couldn't bear to look at Lila. "How long have you known?"

"A few hours. I swear I was going to tell you soon, I just needed to make sure everything with," she paused, not having acknowledged the fact that she was pregnant out loud before, and realized she still couldn't quite. "I don't even know what I'm doing."

Kate shook her head and Lila could see the anger welling up in her, could feel it rolling off her in waves. "You don't know what you're doing, and clearly, neither do I. That was humiliating!"

"Kate, I know, I'm so sorry!"

"No! No, you don't have any idea! Because in a month, no one will even remember who you are, but they'll remember that I was humiliated, that I was caught out on the red carpet, in front of everyone, in front of Wes!"

"You don't mean that."

The limo stopped in front of Lila's building; somehow, there were already photographers waiting. "Please get out," Kate managed through clenched teeth.

"Don't do this, Kate, please," Lila whispered through tears.

Tears spilled from Kate's eyes as well, but her tone was cold. "It's done."

Lila swallowed, nodded silently, and stepped out of the limo and back into the dismal reality of life without the woman she loved.

Kate turned to face Jenna, only to find her assistant glaring at her. "Why are you looking at me as if I've done something wrong?" Kate asked.

"Because that sounded like Wes; it sounded cruel, and that is something you are not."

Kate didn't want to hear it. She wanted to be allowed her rage. But really, she wasn't mad at Lila, but the situation, and of course that bastard Wes. Why couldn't he just leave her alone? She didn't want him! She'd told him that in her studio. How could he possibly think that his actions would do anything but push her further away? She shook her head, just like she'd pushed Lila away. *Fuck!*

"I just want to go home," Kate muttered.

"I don't think that's a good idea," Jenna's phone lit up, and she held it out so Kate could see her publicist Kelli's name.

Kate groaned and leaned her head against the cool glass of the window, watching the lights of the city blaze by.

She heard Jenna muttering to Kelli, saw her assistant nodding her head in silent acceptance or approval several times before she realized Jenna had said her name multiple times.

Kate snapped her attention back to Jenna. "Sorry, what?"

"We're going to the airport. You're going to Jackson to wait this out."

"Like hell I am!"

"Fine then, Scotland, you can walk around and look at pretty things and feed the sheep, or whatever it is you do there!" Jenna was exasperated.

"They're cows, Jenna, Highland cows."

Jenna shot her an annoyed look. "Neither one of us is going to let you slink back to your apartment here and go back into hiding! I haven't wanted to say anything, but the past few years have been like *bloody* Grey Gardens. All we needed was a raccoon and a house boy! I'm not letting you go back into your hole! At least you have your studio out there, you can paint, ride..."

"Be utterly alone."

"You've been alone here!"

"I've had you!"

"I am not a substitute for an actual relationship and you know that. I have my own life outside of cleaning up your messes."

"No, you don't."

"Well, I would if you would start acting like the adult you are!"

Kate sighed. She knew Jenna was right about everything. "This is quite a mess, isn't it?"

"Not impossible to come back from though," she raised a brow in consternation. "Kelli is, of course, already on damage control. I'm partially to blame, I suppose. Wes shouldn't have gotten anywhere near you. I'm sorry."

"Would things have gone any differently had I found out about Lila in private? I don't know why I ever thought I could make the relationship work. I feel so stupid, going around like a besotted teenager."

Jenna didn't respond. She knew her boss enough to know, like most artists, she needed to feel those lows before she could feel the highs. She was shocked that Lila was pregnant, but she also knew Kate had wanted kids, so she didn't see a genuine reason that this should end the relationship, unless Kate couldn't get out of her own head.

Kate had her loyalty, but not to her own detriment, not anymore. Lila had been good for Kate, and after getting to know her, Jenna admitted she liked her and wanted them to work out. Jenna missed that dazzling woman that it seemed Lila had seen, even when Kate had lost sight of her herself. She wasn't about to let Kate throw this relationship away on a whim.

"Give me one night," Kate said, "to feel sorry for myself. I'll go to Jackson tomorrow afternoon, ok?"

Jenna's eyes narrowed, trying to decide if her boss was planning an escape. "You promise?"

"Promise."

There was nowhere safe now in Lila's tiny apartment; every corner now housed a memory of Kate; the bed still held the scent of orange blossom and rose associated with her. Every time she glimpsed the small galley kitchen, she saw Kate standing there in one of her t-shirts and nothing else.

Decisions were going to have to be made. Lila ran a hand over her still flat stomach and sighed. "Not your fault you're causing so much trouble," she spoke to the growing bit of cells within her; she was going to keep it. That was the only thing she knew.

Lila didn't know how long she'd been asleep, but the water was running cold as she woke on the shower floor. She jerked her head up with a start; must have cried herself to sleep. As bad as things were at the moment, she was thankful not to have drowned because of stupidity. She hauled herself out, wrapped a towel around herself and picked up the phone;

several missed calls and texts, but none from the one person she cared about. There was nothing from Kate.

The clock on her phone told her it was still early, not yet even midnight, so she hadn't been out for too long. The reflection staring back at her in the buzzing light of her tiny bathroom was a bedraggled mess; mascara staining her eyes and cheeks black. She didn't even bother washing it off. She was too tired. Too tired of screwing up, too tired of feeling like she wasn't good enough for anybody, let alone Kate. And now, knowing that she was pregnant, it made sense why she was just plain tired.

Lila didn't want to talk to many people right now, but Liz was one of them and she was grateful when she saw her friend's name pop up on her phone without her having to make the call.

"I know it's a stupid question," Liz started as Lila picked up, "but are you ok?"

"No, I'm not ok," she responded, "but I appreciate you asking."

"Should I come over?"

"No, there were already paparazzi outside when I got home. And, I think I just need to wallow in my misery alone for a while."

"I guess Kate isn't with you then?"

"Nope, I'm not sure I'll be seeing her again." There, the thought that had been spiraling about in her mind had finally been said aloud.

"I'm really sorry. I wouldn't give up just yet though; you said you two talked about kids."

"In the extreme, put my foot in my mouth, hypothetical sort of way."

"Well, have you figured out what to do about Phillip?"

"I'm going to have to tell him. No matter what, I don't want him popping back up in my life and trying to take the baby away."

"You think he'd do that?"

"I don't know. One of his friends got a girl pregnant, and they ended up getting married even though they weren't in love. He told me he thought that was noble. I think I'd rather be single than with someone just because we were too drunk to remember a condom."

"You absolutely cannot marry him!"

"I swear, I'm not planning on it!" She drew an 'x,' over her heart and smiled. "I don't think he'd ever try to hurt me, but, he may want to be in the kid's life, which, I guess I'd be ok with."

"You don't sound so sure."

"I'm not sure how you can be in this kind of situation. Phillip isn't a bad guy, just a flakey one."

"Flakey isn't good for a kid, you know that."

Liz was referencing Lila's mother, and Lila knew it. "I wouldn't call my mom flakey, just self-absorbed to the degree of sometimes forgetting she has a daughter while at other times trying to micromanage my life."

"Right." Liz remembered a certain time when Lila had called her crying because her mom had forgotten to pick her up from school. "What if you and Kate were together? Would you still tell Phillip?"

"Not that it is an issue now, but yeah."

"It sounds like you've decided to keep it, at the very least."

"I think so, but Liz, what about the drinking? What if I've harmed the baby?"

"You've stopped now, I'm assuming?"

"Of course."

"Then that's all you can do. Talk to your doctor, but I think the vast majority of women out there probably had a few drinks before they knew they were pregnant. My cousin got pregnant at a Con, so, I think you should be fine."

"I know, but I'm so worried I've already screwed it up!"

"I'm pretty sure you're going to be thinking that for the rest of your life now that you're going to be a mom. Fuck, that's weird to say!"

"Thanks for the pep talk."

"Sure thing. Ok, let me know how everything goes when you talk to him and any developments with you and Kate. I love you, ok?"

"Love you too, friend." Lila hung up and squeezed her eyes tight, trying to block out reality for just a second. It was going to be a very long couple of days.

———

Kate was pacing in her apartment, having finally gotten rid of Jenna after swearing on her mother's grave that she would stay put until the morning. God! She felt like an idiot! She hated to admit it, even to herself, but she had really dared to hope that just maybe, she and Lila were going to work out. They'd been through that first horrible fight and makeup. Her darkest secrets had been broadcast to the public, but now it appeared she may have finally lost the one person who made it worthwhile.

She needed time though; having a child, being a mother, they were thoughts that, over the last few years, had come to mind more and more often. Nevertheless, there were so many moving pieces to untangle before she could decide. And ultimately, it wasn't even up to her; Lila held all the cards here, and it was for her to decide the next steps. Yes, Kate was embarrassed, but she knew it was Wes that she should be, and was angry at, not Lila. Of course she'd been angry in the moment, but the heat of that gut reaction had worn off and now she wished she could go to Lila and tell her that all would be well, even though she knew it may not be.

———

Lila emailed her boss early in the morning and used a precious sick day, and could tell by the quick response that the woman was glad Lila wouldn't be in. She'd been up most of the night. After she'd talked to Liz, she'd thrown her phone into the corner of the room and tried to not give it a second thought; she'd spent more time than she'd care to admit staring a hole into the space where her phone had landed. Of course, she couldn't get her mind on anything else. Lila was in a panic. She knew that her face and video of the incident on the red carpet were everywhere. She knew Kate was humiliated. Lila knew Wes was a total psycho, who wouldn't stop until she and Kate's relationship was destroyed.

As the sun rose, she finally drifted into a fitful sleep. It was midmorning by the time she woke and decided she had to face the day and the world. An email address stood out amongst the morning spam; it was Phillip's. The subject read simply but in bold, "IS IT MINE?" Of course this was going to have happened, but why now? Lila wanted to stay in her pit of misery, eating ice cream and watching old movies for at least one day. The universe wasn't even giving her that. With bile forming at the base of her throat, she opened the email. There was simply a phone number.

There was loud music and voices in the background as Phillip picked up. "Let me call you back in just a second!" Was all Lila could hear shouted over the din on the other end. It had sounded like a bar, which meant he must be back in Singapore, there being a twelve hour time difference.

She hung her head in her hands, waiting for her phone to ring as if awaiting the executioner. Though expected, she jumped as less than two minutes later, it rang; the screen showing Phillip's name.

"Hey," she said.

"You sound tired," came the familiar voice. "You doing ok?"

They'd never been enemies, never had a real quarrel, they'd simply not been right for each other. So now, as Phillip spoke, she was happy as she could be to hear his voice.

"I'm alright," she nearly sobbed, but was able to swallow it; crying would do no good now.

"I'm sure that's not true."

"No, it's not, but nothing to be done for it now. How are you?" There was something very comforting in the banal banter.

"Well, since you're calling me, I'm guessing I'm the one to blame for your situation."

"There were two of us in that bed."

"Yeah, well, I'm sorry, I guess?"

There was honking in the call's background, a few angry shouts. Lila could picture him, hand nervously brushing his hair this way and that as he paced the neon-lit streets of Singapore.

"I was happy for you, you know," Phillip said, "when I saw pictures of the two of you together. I never wanted to hurt you, but I knew I couldn't be what you needed and deserved."

"I know," she whispered, still not trusting her voice. "I think I really fucked that up, though. I don't see how she can trust me after this. Or, if she even wants a kid; one that's not hers."

"If you keep this baby, I just want you to know that I'll do everything I can to help you, and be there as much or as little as you want."

She wasn't angry with him, just sad. She didn't want to be with Phillip anymore, but she also wasn't about to let him string a kid along like he had her. "Being there has never been one of your strong suits."

"You're right, and I know you and I won't work as a couple, but I want you to know that in my way, I'm here. I just really hope you and Kate can work things out. You looked really happy with her."

"I don't want to lose her, but I don't know what to do."

"You'll get through this. I know you will. I don't know anyone more resilient than you."

"Thanks. I really needed that right now."

Lila hung up with Phillip and felt, if not happy, somewhat relieved; he wouldn't get in her way or try to come between her and Kate should they ever get back together. And there were no more secrets from anybody, not that she had kept hers for long. Still, having it out made it seem less scary.

She was scrubbing her face when her call box buzzed. *Great, I've got zero interest in being cheered up today.* She assumed it was Liz as she was her only real friend in the city, or, god forbid, a reporter. Turns out, being called out for hiding a pregnancy on the red carpet by your girlfriend's ex is the stuff a tabloid writer's dreams are made of as she found out from news that she and Kate were once again trending on Twitter.

She dried her face off, then slogged to the call box. "Who is it?"

"It's me," came the smokey English accent on the other end. It was Kate.

Lila leaned her head against the wall, not daring to hope that she had shown up to make up. Lila was expecting a fight and, if she were being honest with herself, she was almost welcoming one. "Come up," she said, buzzing Kate in.

"Jenna and Kelli don't know I'm here," she said as Lila opened the door. "I'm supposed to be packing."

"You're leaving?"

"Just for a few days. Kelli seems to think it's the best course."

Kate looked like her night had been as miserable as her own, Lila thought. Dark circles rimmed tired looking green eyes. Her hair was squashed under a baseball cap and she'd forgone her usual jeans for yoga pants. Lila had wanted to yell at her, even though she'd caused Kate's anger; Kate had been cruel in the car as they'd left the benefit; said things that Lila's brain kept coming back to. But seeing her look as much a mess as she no doubt did herself, made Lila want to take pity on the love of her life, standing there in her hallway.

"The Paparazzi are finally gone then?" Lila relented before she'd even begun; she didn't want their relationship to be one of continuous angry blowups. If they were going to have any hope, they were both going to have to start listening to each other and be grown-ups.

"Looks like it. Guess we're old news."

"I doubt that; have you seen the internet?" Lila asked.

"Not if I can help it," Kate smiled wanly. "May I come in for a minute? You can say no, of course. I wouldn't blame you if you slammed the door in my face, but, I hope you don't."

Lila struggled with herself. She didn't want to hope, but if Kate was leaving, they definitely needed to talk. "Sure, come in," she said, stepping aside and letting Kate in.

As soon as the door was closed, Kate spun, and spoke. "Lila," her eyes were shut, trying to keep the tears from spilling, "I know you weren't trying to hurt me, but I need some time. It's just," she paused, ran a hand over her face, "God, I don't know what I was expecting from this relationship, but it wasn't this." She took a breath and dared a look.

"Me either. Definitely wasn't planning on being a mom anytime soon," Lila shook her head. "I get it, I do. We've been nothing but drama from day one; I'm sure you're tired of that, especially after everything else you've been through. I'm going to get out of town for a while too." She hadn't known until the words were out of her mouth that she was indeed leaving. Lila didn't want to; she felt like she'd just settled back into the city, into her job, and here she was, running away. But now, looking at Kate, she knew she couldn't be in the same city without losing her mind, and likewise, if Kate was leaving, what was the point of staying? "I don't think I can be here without you," she said miserably, shocked by her own forthrightness. Her inner voice piped up, *A tad melodramatic, isn't it? You're not in an Austen novel.*

Panic roiled Kate's stomach. She didn't know if there was a future with Lila or not, but the thought of her being out of reach scared her. "Where are you going?"

"My parents have a place at Lake Arrowhead. I'm sure they won't mind if I camp out there for a while."

"But, what about your job? Your apartment?"

Lila smiled and shrugged. "I'll figure it out; I always do."

Kate knew she really needed time to sit with all of it; the pregnancy, the age difference, not to mention her own life, but all she wanted to do was reach out, pull Lila to her and tell her to stay, or better yet, come with her. But she didn't, because she knew it wasn't right, not yet, or if it ever would be.

"Is this goodbye then?" Lila didn't want it to be; Kate's being here had made her desire for her, her love for her even more real.

Kate tried to smile as she swallowed her tears. "I don't know, but, maybe." She wrapped her arms around Lila and pulled her close, burying her face in the crook of Lila's neck. Lila could feel the wetness of the tears against her skin as she too held tight and cried for what could be the loss of her love.

———

It was her dad's rarely used number Lila punched into her phone from the airport. She didn't talk to him nearly as much as she should, and then when she thought about calling him, she felt guilty that she hadn't in so long, and so she would put the call off yet again. Now, though, she didn't know who else to call. As bad as admitting defeat and coming home, tail tucked between her legs, so to speak, it was nothing to feeling as though she had lost Kate. But defeated, she was. She'd lost her job, her home, and the love of her life in one fell swoop. And there was nothing about it that was not her own fault or her own decision.

Her father had wrapped her in a warm hug when he picked her up outside the terminal; whispered, "You'll get through this," against her ear. It felt like a lifetime since she'd seen him and now she was coming home like this, out of work, knocked up, humiliated.

"Your mom wanted to come."

She looked over at her dad, startled. "How did you manage to dissuade her?"

"I told her 'no'." He put the car in drive and started off. Lila was shocked. She didn't remember her dad ever saying no to her domineering mother. "I didn't think you needed any more stress in your life right now."

The emotion was apparent in her voice when she said, "Thanks dad, seriously."

He looked over and gave her a brief smile. "You're not alone in this, ok?"

"Ok," she nodded. The two remained silent for the remainder of the almost two-hour drive.

———

Lila tried to settle into the new monotonous existence of an exile. She wandered the house, occasionally went grocery shopping, poked around the tourist shops of the town. She didn't want to stay in Arrowhead; she knew that, but she didn't want to go back to New York, either. The city had already begun to lose its charm before she and Kate got together, and the thought of trying to navigate it with a child in tow was one of sheer dread; the image of hauling a stroller up and down subway steps alone was enough to cause her to break out in a cold sweat.

She didn't know what her next step was or who, if anyone, it was going to involve. What she knew was that she missed Kate with every damn fiber of her being.

# 27

Kate followed the advice of Jenna and Kelli; she went away. She spent three weeks trying to pretend. Three weeks trying to nuke her and Lila's relationship in her mind, because that would be easier than trying to repair it. At least, that's what she kept telling herself.

Lila's life would be easier and better without her in it, wouldn't it? She was mercurial after all; a temperamental artist. But, for every time she told herself that, she would also think of the way Lila made her feel. She made her feel like she was finally home, like she was grounded in the best way possible.

Jules hugged her friend tight. This was the first time she'd seen her since the red carpet debacle, and worried didn't begin to cover what she was feeling; Kate looked terrible, like she hadn't slept in the weeks she'd been apart from Lila. She took a deep breath before speaking. "I'm not a potstirrer, you know that," she said as they plopped down on her sofa, "and I hate unsolicited advice, but, do you want mine?"

Kate's head was in her hands. She hadn't known where else to go or what else to do other than go back to New York. Being away from the city had been no help whatsoever and Jules was the one person in her life in a functional relationship that really knew her. "It's over, right? The other shoe always drops, doesn't it? And this is it. I should have listened to her. Life is a bunch of bullshit and in the end you're alone."

Jules pulled away, "Ok, now you're getting this unsolicited advice speech because you're being melodramatic as fuck and I've already been cried and snoted on by a melodramatic girl once today, and she was 4." Kate looked up, eyes and nose streaming. "You're still not a pretty crier, you know," Jules scoffed. Kate couldn't argue with that. She could feel her swollen lips and eyes.

"So I've been told," she grumbled.

"Life is a bunch of bullshit," Jules started again, "but it's also a lot of really amazing things too. And having a kid, being a parent, is the same. You're not going into this totally blind. You survived for a week at the beach with my hoard. You know it's hard and exhausting and hell on a relationship, but for me, it's worth it. No, it isn't for everyone and not all relationships survive it. But, for as long as I've known you, which is longer than either of us cares to admit, family is what you've wanted. Yeah, you've made a great one with your friends, but you've wanted to be a mom for a while now. You've always wanted to give a kid what you didn't get to have with your mom. And now, you have a chance. And, it's a chance to do it with someone you love; you won't be alone in this." Jules nudged Kate, who ceased sobbing and was sniffling quietly as her friend spoke. "You won't even have stretch marks, you bitch," Jules smiled.

Kate grabbed a tissue and swiped at her nose. "You don't have stretch marks," she said, returning the smile, even if it didn't reach her eyes. "I don't even know if Lila's keeping it. I, I didn't even ask, I just shut down. I don't know anything."

"You know how you feel about her though, don't you."

"About Lila?" Kate breathed, closed her eyes. "Yeah, yeah I do. And I know what I think I want. But, what if she doesn't, she's twenty-seven, what if she doesn't want to settle down? It's asking a lot of her."

"You never should have ended up with Wes."

"What does he have to do with it?"

"You've never been with someone who gives you all of themselves; its always been you giving up what you want to make something work for someone else. Before you found out about the baby, what were your plans with Lila?"

"You know I wanted to marry her, to be with her."

"And she wanted to be with you. So now, even if there's no baby, wouldn't you still want to be with her?"

"Didn't you just tell me I wanted to be a mother more than anything?"

"I said you wanted a family. You and another person together against the world. It's what you tried to have with Wes, but he was never that guy. He's always been all about himself, and you know it. But with Lila, before all this, it was the two of you together, against all the rest of it. And baby, or no baby, it still can be. Though I do hope there's a baby because I totally want to spoil the shit out of your kid."

Kate sighed. "I need to go pack, don't I?"

"It's not my choice, but I think you should."

"Me too!" came a man's voice from the hall.

"Luke!" both women shouted as Jules' husband came around the corner, a sheepish look on his face.

"Sorry, I didn't want to interrupt," he looked at Kate, "but you know she's going to tell me everything, anyway."

"Not if she told me not to!" Jules defended herself.

Luke held his hands up. "Ok, that's true."

Kate shook her head and stood. She gave Jules a hug and Luke one as well before picking her coat up from the arm of the sofa. "I love you guys. Thanks."

As the door closed behind Kate, Luke swept Jen into a tight bear hug, smiled down into her eyes, and kissed her. "So, you told her to go after the girl, huh?"

She grinned back. "Good advice?"

"Definitely!"

———

Kate stepped from the plane, shivered; the cool air of a California Fall evening whirled around her. *You've got this*, she told herself as she slid into the worn upholstery of the rental car and headed off towards the small resort town.

She wasn't sure what she'd say when she got there; wasn't even sure what she'd find. She and Lila had been apart for only three weeks, but as they'd found out, it only took thirty seconds for your life to change.

Lila couldn't speak as she stood at the door, unblinking, unable to make a move. Kate stood before her, like something out of a ridiculous romcom, soaked from the pouring rain; luggage dropped by her side.

Kate smiled tentatively. "I don't suppose I could bother you for a cup of tea?"

Lila finally woke from her startled trance; Kate Manderly was the last person on earth she'd expected when she opened the door. But she was pleased, so very pleased that it took her a second more to respond. "I think that's the most English thing you've ever said to me," she grinned back and stepped out of Kate's way, motioning her into the snug cabin.

Kate stepped inside, a puddle of water instantly forming at her feet.

"What's with the wet grand gesture? Isn't it slightly over the top?"

"Worked the first time," Kate smiled, and Lila sighed. There was no point anymore in even trying to pretend she could be anything but hopelessly in love with this woman. And, it was true, Lila didn't think there was a thing she couldn't forgive Kate for if she showed up looking for all the world like Marianne Dashwood, half drowned on her doorstep. Kate sure as hell wasn't wrong about it working the first time, and from the way Lila's stomach was turning somersaults and her heart was racing, she was certain it was going to work the second time too.

"Let me get you a towel," Lila said and dashed off. Kate was here! Kate was here and didn't seem mad, at least in the fifteen seconds of interaction they had. What did it mean? Why was she here? Lila's mind was racing as she tried to nonchalantly face Kate again, towel in outstretched hand.

"Thanks." Kate took the proffered towel and went to work on the mass of bedraggled, dripping curls.

Lila stood by anxiously. "No problem," she said, turning her face away as Kate dropped the towel and stripped off her wet sweater, revealing her goddess-like figure beneath.

Kate caught the movement and laughed. "Nothing you haven't seen before," she said, winking and peeling her jeans down her legs. Lila unconsciously groaned; as always, Kate was sans underwear.

"God," Lila said, perching on the arm of an ancient flannel covered sofa, "you best be flirting with me woman, otherwise this is just cruel and unusual!"

Kate deftly flipped the towel up to her hands with a toe, wrapped it around her waist, and sauntered towards Lila, hips swaying, a wicked smirk on her full lips. "I didn't come all this way to just have a conversation."

Lila felt her stomach flip again in excitement as Kate reached her, ran her hands up her back, through her hair, leaning in for a hungry kiss. Lila leaned into the kiss; the scent and touch and taste of Kate flooding through her. She wanted to give herself over to the moment, to let Kate take what she would from her; Lila paused. It wasn't just her now. It never would be ever again.

If Kate was here for her, for them, Lila had to know. Because, if she wasn't, if this was just some last tryst before getting on with her life, Lila wanted nothing to do with it. Well, that was what she was trying to tell herself as her hand slid the towel from around Kate's waist. She couldn't just act as if her actions had no consequences anymore; that's how she'd ended up pregnant, after all.

"Wait," Lila said, pulling from the tight embrace. "I need you to know I'm keeping the baby." Her eyes searched Kate's, and she smiled as she saw them light with joy, an echoing smile coming to her lips.

"And I'm here for it, for all of it; for you, for the baby. I love you. I won't lie that I'm not terrified by the thought of being a mother, but I do want to try. With you." She brushed her thumb over Lila's cheek. "I love you so much," she said as she leaned back into the embrace, their foreheads touching, their breath mingling.

Tears of relief spilled from Lila's eyes as her arms once again went around Kate's waist. "I love you too," she mumbled, as their lips crashed against each other.

Kate's impulse was to throw Lila back onto the sofa; a fast, rough reunion, but she stopped herself. "I don't want to hurt you," she rasped.

Lila was unbuttoning her pajama top, wishing she was wearing something sexier for this moment. "You won't," she breathed, "you can't." She was out of her shirt now, her hips pressing into Kate's, her fingers pressing into Kate's flesh, keeping them melded together even as she pushed them back towards the bedroom.

———

Lila's finger twitched, the first inkling of her waking body. Something was tickling her nose; Kates's wild hair; her lover's beautiful, curling, wild red hair. Still on the edge of waking, Lila smiled and snuggled in even closer to the warmth of the woman in her embrace. She sensed the corresponding smile on Kate's lips as the other woman's fingers slipped between hers, and she heard a satisfied little moan of contentment.

She wondered if Kate could feel her heart beating fast against her back; answering each rapid beat with her own. This was what she'd been after her entire life; this sense of peace and belonging. What she had kept trying to make a reality with Phillip, had fallen so easily into place with Kate.

Besides Phillip, Lila had always been the one to pull back in a relationship, not that she'd had many "real" ones. But it had always been her aloofness that caused the breakup. She had always held her heart for herself. With Kate, she had known, even in her excited, drunken stupor, that her heart was safe with her. Yes, that first morning had been a bit of a mess. She hadn't been able to believe anything other than she had found the one person in the universe she was meant to be with.

"Any chance we can magically make coffee and breakfast appear?" Kate grumbled.

"Ha, don't think so."

"Pity," Kate guided Lila's hand to her breast, "guess we'll just have to distract ourselves all morning. I'm not leaving this bloody bed."

"Guess so." Lila's hand gave Kate's breast an appreciative squeeze before gliding down the tautness of her stomach, sliding into the soaked folds of her pussy. "Somebody's excited," Lila murmured happily.

"I've been very neglected as of late," she groaned as Lila's fingers stroked and entered her.

Lila's lips were hard against hers. "I won't let it happen again," she managed.

————

Kate was lit like a Vermeer in the frosty morning light. Her bare golden legs were tucked up under her as she scribbled in a notebook. A log popped in the wood burning fire. Kate took the reading glasses from the tip of her nose, tilted her head back, eyes closed, and stretched. Her arms raised languidly heavenward, a contented smile gracing her lips.

Lila didn't dare breathe; she'd never forgive herself if she shattered the tranquil bliss of the moment, the seemingly unstudied contentedness of her love.

"Like what you see?" came Kate's teasing voice, startling Lila.

"Pretty sure you know I do," she laughed and came to sit on the floor by Kate, resting her chin on Kate's shoulder. "What're you doing?"

Kate held the tiny notebook up for her to see. "Working on a list of things I need to sort when I get back."

Lila sighed. "Guess we can't stay here forever."

"No, I don't think so. But, I've been thinking; I don't need to be in New York anymore, especially not after the show is over with."

"You want to leave New York? You love it there, I love it there, sort of, when I'm with you." She had loved it, certainly had back in grad-school, but things hadn't felt the same since she'd been back. Maybe Kate was right, maybe it was time to leave the Big Apple behind, but what did Kate have in mind?

"I'm done, with all of it."

"All of what?"

"The bullshit. The endless parties, the schmoozing, the smell, the noise; all of it!"

"You don't mean that, Kate."

"I do, I mean, of course I'll still paint, but I want to do it because it's what I want to do, not because of some deadline or because I need more money, because, thank god, I don't. You're what inspires me now; you, our life together. I was so lost for so long. I was terrified that I'd never find myself again. But with you, I know exactly who I am, exactly what I want. I don't want a life full of people who only care about what I can give them or how they can use me. And I don't want our child to be raised in that either. I want her to have the freedom to be whoever she is."

Lila couldn't help but break into a wide grin as Kate spoke. "Our child?"

"I told you, I'm here for it, you, and her." She moved, opening her arms, embracing Lila, who was all too happy to snuggle into the warmth of her girlfriend.

"You seem very certain it's a girl."

"That's because she is. I know these things," she winked and Lila did not doubt the creature before her had more than a little magic running through her veins. She kissed Lila's shoulder, only her eyes visible above their line as she muttered glumly, "I just wish we could stay here." The little fire in the wood stove popped, the smell of wood-smoke and coffee swirling around them.

Lila didn't want to leave either, but she knew that for the moment, at least, their real lives needed their attention. There was some major cleaning up that had to be addressed before they could get on with what she hoped would be their happily ever after.

"I wish we could stay here too," she responded, soaking in the calm, coziness of their surroundings, "well," she amended, "not here, here," this place did after all hold too many unpleasant memories of her mother and awkward family gatherings, "but definitely away with you."

"What do you think of Wyoming?" Kate asked.

That brought Lila out of her drowsy reverie. "I don't think about it at all, truth be told." She gave Kate a sideways glance. "Let me guess, you know a place?"

Kate chuckled, "You've got me!" she nudged Lila playfully.

"It's so weird to try to put the pieces of you together. Like, I just never would have imagined the first time I met you, all decked out in your penthouse, that you're constantly trying to run off to some out of the way, rustic hideout."

"It's the highlander in me. Just wasn't cut out for city living. My gran always said my blood was too wild."

"She had you pegged, that's for sure."

"Not too wild for you, though?" She cocked a brow, her lip quirked invitingly.

"Not yet."

"Better be not ever." She sighed, "There is something I wanted to ask you."

"What's for breakfast?" Lila teased.

"Will you be my date? For my show. I'd be honored to have you by my side on the biggest night of my life."

Lila blushed as she did some quick math and realized she'd be almost eight months pregnant by then. "Not sure what I'll fit in," she laughed, "but yes, of course!"

"Ok, last question, I promise!"

"Shoot."

"Will you move in with me?"

Lila feigned shock, even though the eventuality of their cohabitation, especially if they were raising a child together, seemed inevitable. Still, she was flattered. "Leave my airless, lightless studio for a glamorous penthouse, you mean?"

"I do."

"I guess I can make that happen." Lila kissed Kate, stared into those sparkling sea glass eyes. "I guess we're even more super official than we were."

Kate laughed. "Yes, super official."

# 28

"This is one of the first Thanksgivings I haven't been home for," Lila said as they sat, watching the Thanksgiving Parade on TV, not having any desire to be out in the half frozen crowds themselves.

"I'm sorry, love, I should have insisted we go!" Kate said, shifting Lila's weight on her as they sat huddled together on the living room sofa. "I thought you were trying to avoid your mother and quite frankly, I've never enjoyed her company and I'm certain she's not going to be any more approving of me now that I've made off with her daughter. I could get the plane though, we could be there for dinner!"

"No! Seriously!" Lila dropped a gentle kiss onto Kate's lips, a groan from Kate meeting their touch. "I want to eat a ridiculous amount of Chinese food, stay in my pajamas and cuddle with you all day! Drama free! Best Thanksgiving ever!"

"Well, I can't promise drama free," Kate said, "but, I'll try."

217

Living with Kate was easy, Lila found. Yes, she was an eccentric, melodramatic artist, but she seemed to reserve most of that for her studio and her actual art, which she was finally getting back on track with. And Lila found that living with Kate meant even on those evenings when they both fell exhausted onto the sofa or bed, the delight in each other's presence was still undeniable.

After they returned from California, it was a quick shift for Lila; she left her job permanently, she couldn't be around the chemicals used while pregnant, and as they'd decided to move after the baby was born; Lila spent most of her time contemplating what this new life meant.

She was, in essence, giving up the career she had just begun, and was still trying to come to terms with the fact while also still trying to figure out what being a mother would mean. Hers was a terrible example whom she had no desire to emulate, and Kate lost hers at a young age.

They were both stressed, but coping and learning to lean on each other, a skill that Jules told them, was essential to survive parenthood. But, even with Kate doting on her, Lila couldn't help but suffer from bouts of ennui brought on by her inability, for the time being, to indulge her talents. However, there was no understating the relief they were both finding in the calm routine of their new life together. There were no more soul crushing revelations, no blow ups; everything seemed blissfully normal in a way that Lila and Kate had both always wanted.

"Well, we can go…" Kate's voice dropped off.

"What were you going to say?" Lila asked dejectedly.

"Skiing," Kate grumbled. She was having a very hard time convincing Lila that her pregnancy wasn't becoming an inconvenience, because the truth was that yes, it was causing her to change her lifestyle. But she had to make Lila believe she was doing so willingly. She wasn't some ensnared, helpless woman. She was very much in control of her own life, now more so than ever, and she was making the choice to be with Lila and their child.

"We could drive upstate, get a cabin, sip cocoa, have sex in front of a fire."

Lila cocked her head, studying her love. "It's just us, isn't it?"

"What do you mean?"

"Us, against the world. I mean, neither one of us is close with their family, and our friends all have their own things, own families."

Kate's mood brightened. "It's hardly Oliver Twist," she laughed.

"When my grandmother was alive," Lila started, "every holiday was a huge event with tons of food and cousins running all over the place, but after she died, my mom just didn't care; we'd go to the club or something, then get away from each other as fast as possible. It just became more sad than anything."

"And you're upset thinking about our child growing up without all that? The food and cousins, etc.?"

"Honestly, I don't really even like my cousins; it's better now that we're adults, but, they made my life hell as kids, I was always the littlest."

"But the feistiest, I have no doubt," she winked. "If you want our kid to have big, crazy holidays we'll make it happen, and if you want us to hop on a plane and get the hell away from everyone else, we can do that too. I think the best thing we can do is not try to place all kinds of expectations on our life. We're together. Period. Let the chips fall where they may."

The apartment's buzzer sounded. "Chinese food," Kate beamed.

———

Lila was snuggled deep in her favorite blanket on the living room sofa as the first fog of winter obscured the views of skyscrapers outside the windows of the apartment she now considered home. Lila left Kate in bed, still deep asleep almost an hour before; she was just reaching the stage of pregnancy where her condition was taking its toll on her sleep, and she found she could never sleep in anymore, being uncomfortable in just about every position. She could still hide her pregnancy in the right clothes, but the baby was making its presence known in the ever growing little bump of her belly and her swollen breasts, which both she and Kate already decided they would miss terribly.

Jenna arrived and was making coffee. Over the last few months, the tiny, frosty exterior of the English woman thawed towards Lila, and Lila found herself grateful for the friendship. She half suspected that Kate originally put Jenna up to keeping her entertained during the day; while Kate was at the studio working on pieces for the show, Jenna would take her to lunch, go to the movies with her, or stroll through the halls of various museums, but Lila was sure Jenna genuinely liked her now. And that was something. In the new world she found herself in with Kate, unless Jules and Luke were around, she still felt like an interloper, so having Jenna on her side was a bonus.

She was sipping on her hot chocolate, desperately wishing it was the coffee she could smell brewing in the kitchen, when she heard Kate behind her.

"Who turned the damn news on?" Kate asked, irritated. She'd been avoiding it as much as possible ever since Wes started showing up on it. And besides, it was far too early in the morning to endure the grating voices of the reporters.

Lila hadn't registered that the TV was even on; she was currently engrossed in a gory True Crime podcast while wandering through the contents of the internet on her phone. She looked up at Kate's question to see the image of Kate's ex's good-looking, tanned face staring back at her from the screen.

"It's Wes!" Jenna sounded oddly cheery about it as she popped her head in from the kitchen. "His hearing is scheduled this morning; kind of wanted to see his perp walk," she said. And there he was, perfectly dressed and relaxed looking, white teeth shining in that handsome face of his.

He looked as cool and collected as ever. Kate's stomach recoiled at the sight of him. The newscaster's voice started speaking over the live footage of Wes and his lawyer entering the courthouse. "Wes Aldridge, financier and ex-husband of artist Kate Manderly..."

"Turn it off, please," Kate said wearily. She could hear all about it later without having to look at that charming facade and hear her name, once again, tied to that man.

Jenna reached for the remote, hitting the power button as the newscaster's voice was droning on as a picture of Kate and Lila, walking down the street, hand in hand, flashed. "Manderly of course has been making her own headlines as of late..." the screen thankfully going black before they had to hear another word.

"This isn't going to come back on you, is it?" Lila asked. In the months they'd been together, Wes' impending trial had been one subject they steered clear of, but now that it was here, and now that they were planning on raising a child together, Lila needed to know.

"The lawyers don't think so, thank god. I'll say this for them, and my sister, they at least had the forethought to keep all finances separate when we got married. It was meant to protect what my parents left me. Now it's going to end up saving my ass."

"The lovely ass that it is," Lila quipped.

"Are you going to have to testify?" asked Jenna.

Kate shrugged. "They haven't asked me too yet, so I guess not, but Wes never told me anything about his business. It never interested me, and I always had enough of my own money to do what I wanted. Never had to take a dime from that man." She had worked for it, too. What her parents left for her was a sizable trust fund that would allow her to be comfortable, but, she hadn't been allowed access to it until she was thirty-five, which, by that time, she'd made her first million many times over.

"Money laundering, securities fraud," Jenna whistled, "over twelve counts! They're saying he could get life."

It was clear by the displeased look on Kate's face that she was done talking about it, so she stopped talking, but gave Lila her own look; Kate might not be in any kind of legal trouble, but there was bound to be fallout from her ex-husband's crimes.

# 29

After Wes started making headlines again with his trial, it was clear that Kate was on edge. More than ever, Lila could see the strain of the city and all that came with it, wearing on her. They'd batted different ideas around, most of them pipe dreams; buying a surf shop in Costa Rica, a vineyard in Italy. Kate had the money, sure, but neither one of them knew what they were doing outside of art. So art was where they landed once again. With the baby arriving and Kate's show on the horizon, it would be the perfect time for them to get away and focus on their shared passion. But the *where*, was still giving Lila heartburn.

———

"I don't know, Liz," Lila had her head in her hands, this was a huge decision, "she doesn't want to be here anymore, and I get that, and I'm not opposed to getting out of the city, but

Wyoming? I feel like I'm more of a quaint fishing village in Maine type of girl. Or even her place in Scotland."

Liz was trying to be understanding, but try as she may, she didn't feel too sorry for her friend. "Yeah, I don't know what I'd do with all that blue sky and fresh air, time and money to do what I actually want instead of what I have to do. Plus a super hot girlfriend. Sucks to be you."

"I can't do shit right now! I'm just trapped in my body, growing another person, being someone famous' girlfriend!" Lila blurted. "Ok," Lila took a breath, realized she sounded a tad bit whiny, "but it's her money, her house. What am I contributing? I didn't sign up to be a kept woman with a baby in tow."

"Love, emotional support, I'm assuming sex," Liz motioned to her friend's burgeoning abdomen, "a baby." Lila had gained little excess weight, and for that she was grateful, but at four and a half months pregnant, there was hardly any hiding it.

"Great," she threw up her hands, "so I'm just going to be some stay at home mom? I didn't go to school for seven years to sit on a couch and change diapers all day! That's not who I am!"

"So, as a former nanny, I can tell you, you may have seriously underestimated what goes into parenting, and if this kid has your ADD and shall we call it, Kate's flare, you're definitely not going to be sitting at all. Also, I don't think that's what Kate is expecting of you. I get the feeling she looks at you as an equal partner in the relationship, and so what if you're not splitting the mortgage with her, or whatever..."

"I don't think she has a mortgage," Lila grumbled. Liz was making some very valid points, but she wasn't yet ready to cede her ground.

Liz was glaring at her, "If you want me to feel sorry because a gorgeous, kind, wonderful, very wealthy woman, that you are madly in love with, wants to financially support you so you can focus on your art instead of spending your life repairing someone else's, then no, can't do it."

"Shit." Lila shook her head, took a sip of her ice water, wishing it was something stronger. "When you say it like that, I sound like an asshole."

Liz nodded, eyes wide, lips pursed. "Yeah," she said, "you kinda do. I know you can't paint right now; I'm sure that's frustrating as hell, especially with Kate spending so much time at the studio, but your life is about to be crazy. I know it's easier said than done and all of that, but just try to enjoy the calm before the storm."

———

No one noticed her entrance, or if they did, Lila's presence in Kate's studio had become so commonplace it no longer merited an acknowledgement. A few interns were whizzing about, another was in the corner on the phone. Kate was off to the side, unconsciously sexy as hell. She was taking what looked like a break, from painting at least; feet tucked under her on the sofa, glasses perched low on her nose, in the little lounge area of the space, a glass of whisky on the table.

"Alright," Lila said, slinging her coat onto the back of the sofa. "I'm in."

Kate jumped a bit, startled, took her reading glasses from her nose, placed them on the coffee table beside her delicious looking glass of whisky, closed the moleskin notebook she was writing in. "What exactly are you 'in' for?" Kate asked suspiciously.

Lila took a deep breath. "The move," she said. "Not forever, maybe, but for now, yeah, I'm in."

Kate clapped her hands together, a wide grin breaking over her face. "Oh, this will be so much fun! I promise!" She leapt off the ground and wrapped Lila in a tight embrace. "Damn! I wish we could go right now! I can't wait for you to see the house. I'll have to make some changes, but all that's easy enough."

"You don't have to change things for me," Lila said, suddenly feeling disheartened; changes to their lives were going to have to be made whether they were ready, and liked it, or not.

"Stop." Kate stood, taking Lila's hands in hers. She could tell at this point when Lila's pregnancy hormones were kicking into overdrive and when she needed to be the calm, rational one. "This is for all of us, ok? I don't want you doing this to placate me or something. If it isn't what you really want, we'll figure something else out. The two of you are the most important things in the world to me now. The three of us are going to be in this together, alright?"

Lila nodded, "It's just a lot."

"I know. I'm sorry I get so excited. I think after this week, I could take some time off. I should be done with the big pieces for the show. Why don't we go out to Jackson, let me show you around and see what you think. It was completely unfair of me to expect you to be ok with picking up and moving your life somewhere you've never even been. I'm sorry," she bit her lip, "I've been talking to my therapist about the impulsivity issue."

Lila finally gave her a smile. "Well, clearly you're not the only one with that problem in this relationship or we wouldn't be about to be parents."

Kate drew close, gently brushing a hand over the bump of Lila's belly. "For which I shall be eternally grateful." Lila blushed, still amazed at the tenderness Kate was capable of; something for which she knew she herself would be eternally grateful for.

———

Lila wasn't overly impressed by the brown, thawing Wyoming ground when they landed. It had been a light snow year, and they arrived between the cozy snow season, and the blooming of the mountains once warmer weather arrived. It was never what one might call lush, but it had a barren beauty all its own.

Kate could sense her girlfriend's disappointment as they drove through the mountain passes towards her house; *their* house, she amended in her mind. "We should have come for Christmas, even with you not being able to ski; I should have shown it to you at its best. Though I love it in the summer too." Lila nodded, lips pursed, clearly not impressed. "Really, usually it's only like this about two months out of the year which is more than I can say for the city."

Lila thought about the cloying stickiness of New York City in the summer, the airless subways, the breezeless streets;

feeling like you could suffocate in the hot air. Winter had a few magical days, when the sky was blue and frost was on the air, but, mostly, it was sludging through icy, wet streets with freezing rain stinging your skin. She certainly wouldn't miss that. Kate's eyes held a worried look, waiting for Lila's approval.

She took a deep breath. "Like I said, anywhere is fine, so long as I'm with you."

Kate gave her a smile, but Lila knew she wasn't convinced, and neither was she. Of course, she wanted to love the place like Kate did; they were planning on spending the next few years here, after all. But so far, she was regretting her decision.

The home, when they came upon it, was beautiful; of course it was, it was Kate's. It was a log cabin type building, but to call it a cabin was to call Versailles a house. The huge timber structure melded into the landscape and spoke of warm fires and nights spent in the hot-tub following a day of skiing. It was nothing that Lila could have ever imagined living in.

———

"Here's my studio." Kate opened a door into a light filled room, quickly shutting it as Lila went for a peek. "Ah! No peeking! Not when there's a birthday around the corner!" She shooed Lila away, leading her to the next room. "And this," she said, "is yours."

Lila's breath caught as Kate opened the heavy wooden door onto a twin of her own studio. One unbroken wall was a solid pane of glass; the view beyond of the mountains was incomparable. Half a dozen easels lay against a wall, canvas, paints, brushes, all were there, ready for her use. Lila marveled at the selection, the care Kate had clearly taken in learning, which she preferred.

"This is too much," she breathed into the space.

"It's not. In fact, if anything, it's selfish. I can't very well have you sneaking into my studio for supplies," she teased, but Lila frowned. "What is it, love? I'm only teasing you, you know I wouldn't mind!"

"Of course you'd mind! I'd mind! But that's not it. It's the most wonderful present anyone has ever given me, and I can't even enjoy it right now."

"I'm an idiot! I didn't even think! I just wanted to surprise you, to make this feel like home as soon as you got here."

"I'm used to a view of a brick wall, so, no matter what, you're ahead of the game."

"That's sweet."

"It's true. And it gives me something to look forward to once my body is my own again."

Kate pulled her back out into the hallway, back towards their bedroom. "One last thing," she said, bringing Lila to yet another closed door, this one directly across from their room. They'd toured the entire house and not once had Kate mentioned the baby, so Lila assumed this was going to be the nursery. She opened the door and found an empty room.

"I know I've told you we can totally redo the house, but I want you to know I mean it. This is your house, and the baby's, not just mine. So, if you're ok with it, I thought you'd like to work on this together? Just you and I?"

"Yeah?" Lila asked.

"Yeah."

She didn't know if it was just hormones or the fact that Kate was making such a concerted effort to make room in her life for her, but Lila couldn't hold back the tears any longer.

"God, I hope those are happy tears," Kate said, embracing her, holding her as tight as the little bump would let her.

"They are, I swear. I finally feel like I'm home."

# 30

Days stretched into weeks of painting the nursery, ordering furniture, getting Lila acquainted with the small town. They flew back and forth to New York several times to finish up work on the show, make arrangements for the big move. Jenna was happy to divide her time between the resort town and the big city.

As the desolate early spring turned into summer, Lila realized she loved their new home, their surroundings; rolling hills intersected by the jagged faces of the Tetons. She was even able to teach Kate a thing or two about the fine art of fly fishing. Her body may be unwieldy at the moment, Lila thought, but before too long, she'd be able to step out of her house, and catch trout for breakfast. She couldn't believe she ever complained about her circumstances. She and Kate were on cloud nine.

---

Kate woke to an empty bed and dead silence. Her hand stretched to the spot where Lila had been sleeping next to her, the emptiness still held her warmth; she hadn't been gone long. She wondered if maybe she'd gone out to pick up some breakfast but it didn't seem likely, they'd restocked for the weekend just yesterday in anticipation of not leaving until wheels up Monday morning; she had to get back to New York for a board meeting.

She got out of bed, pulling on her robe, and spotted Lila's phone, still charging on the bedside table. Kate's heart rate began quickening; what if something happened in the middle of the night, what if something was wrong with Lila or the baby and she'd gotten up and now was somewhere hurt, or worse? "Lila?"

Her voice echoed through the empty home and she felt chills run down her spine, her panic growing as each consecutive room proved empty; the bathroom, the kitchen, the back porch. As the back screen door bounced shut, Kate heard a scream. Her head whipped round to the front yard where the awful sound had come from, and she took off through the house.

Her brows furrowed at the scene she was witnessing; her mouth dropped open and she couldn't move. In the seconds it took for her mind to process what was happening, it was too late.

Wes pulled Lila, kicking and screaming, into the SUV, threw the car into drive, and took off down the gravel drive, tires kicking up rocks as he sped away.

Kate screamed. This couldn't be happening, not when they'd finally been happy. She couldn't stop now though, she knew she had to follow them. Kate tore back through the house, finding her keys still hanging from a hook by the door. She took another second to run back into the bedroom and grab her phone. Kate was dialing 911 as she slammed her car door shut and took off down the driveway in pursuit.

"911, what is your emergency?" Kate heard the calm voice of the emergency operator on the other end as her car's tires met the asphalt of the main road. She paused for a moment before clocking the black tire marks turning left.

"My girlfriend has been kidnapped!" she screamed into the car's bluetooth.

"Ok, I need you to calm down, ma'am," the operator's voice spoke. "where are you?"

Kate tried to slow her breathing. It would do Lila no good if she couldn't communicate or got herself into an accident. She slowed her thoughts enough to tell the woman where she was, which direction she was going in; that she had seen her ex-husband force her girlfriend into a car at gunpoint; that she was pregnant.

The operator seemed mildly alarmed when Kate told her she was in pursuit; she was told to pullover and let the police handle the situation. Like hell she was! Just as she was about to use some choice language, she saw Wes' silver SUV. Her speed increased. Not that she knew what to do, or what she could do, other than the fact that she was determined not to lose sight of the car. What did Wes think could possibly come of this?

They'd been too happy in their bubble, and this was what was coming of it. They'd thrown themselves into their life together in Wyoming. Making the house a home ready to welcome the impending new life they were expecting.

Of course they had heard the news, even out here; Wes had been found guilty and was awaiting sentencing. But god, Kate thought, never had she imagined that his hatred, his desperation, could ever come to this.

**Earlier That Morning...**

Lila had been dreaming of Kate; she always dreamt of Kate. Her girlfriend had been moaning in her dream; the echoes of her pleasure still filled Lila's ears as she felt something hard poking into her ribs. Her eyes opened to the barrel of a gun; Wes' cold blue eyes staring down at her from above. She didn't move, didn't make a sound. He pressed a finger to his lips, ordering her into silence. She could hear Kate's still sleeping soft breaths beside her, and she nodded in compliance.

He had the drop on her; there was little to no chance that should she try to make a run for it, or fight back that either she or Kate would walk away unscathed or even with their lives. She did her best to be quiet, to not make any sudden movements that might startle Wes or wake Kate up; Lila knew Kate would all too willingly sacrifice herself, and she couldn't let that happen.

He smiled cruelly at her as she climbed from the bed and stupidly enough, she found herself glad that she'd opted for a t-shirt and boxers instead of the usual nothing when they'd finally gone to bed the night before. His gaze traveled over her, pausing on the obvious bulge of her belly, then flicked back up to meet her eyes. He motioned with the gun for her to walk, and she did.

"What are you doing here Wes?" she whispered as they reached the kitchen. She was trying to think of a way to get help without endangering Kate, but she also knew that if he got her in a car, there was a high probability that she wasn't making it out alive.

He pushed the gun into her side, pushing her further towards the front door. "I need leverage, my dear, and you're it. I'm not going to prison, and wherever I'm going, Kate's coming with me. She'll do it for you!"

"Wes, please, you know this isn't going to solve anything." He had the door open now, and she could see an unfamiliar suv parked at the edge of the gravel driveway.

He sneered at her. "You're not the first little bitch to try to come between us. Kate's mine, she'll always be mine."

The words clicked in Lila's mind, and she felt a chill run through her. "Cecile," she whispered, and knew she shouldn't have as his eyes hardened. He couldn't possibly be admitting to what she thought he was admitting to, could he? Cecile's death had been a suicide; a drowning, hadn't it? She hadn't known the young woman before she'd met her demise. Kate said she'd been depressed, upset at the news of Kate's engagement. Maybe Kate was wrong.

Genuine fear sparked in Lila, and she felt the urge to resist, rising in her. Her feet slowed and as Wes jostled against her, she slammed him back into the doorframe and ran.

If she could just make it to the main road, she thought, if she could just make it there, she may have a chance. And then the ground went out from under her as her bare feet rolled on a sharp piece of gravel. She landed on her back; the wind knocked out of her. *The baby!* Her mind screamed at her to get up, to move, to run, but as she tried to get to her feet, she screamed in pain as her right ankle buckled under her weight. *No!* She tried again, but as she saw Wes coming full tilt down the drive, she knew she was done.

# 31

Kate's ears pricked up, and she turned her head; for once, the sounds of sirens were welcome. Then she heard the sickening crunch of metal. The brakes pumped beneath her as she stomped on the pedal; the car skidding to a stop a dozen yards from the wreckage of Wes' SUV.

Kate could see the lights of police cars coming down the mountain road, but she couldn't wait. The SUV lay on its side. She could see the shattered glass and thick powder in the air from the air bags deploying. An image of her mother, dying, blood bubbling from her lips, shot through Kate's mind as she vaulted from the car.

A figure tumbled through the empty windshield, bloodied and covered in white dust; Lila. Kate felt her stomach drop. She was alive.

"Kate!" Lila screamed as she hobbled towards her. Her feet were bloody, torn from the gravel and asphalt; she didn't care.

She didn't feel a thing except for relief that she was out of that car; the car she'd crashed because there was no other choice. And then she saw Kate's eyes go wide, her mouth open as if to scream. There was a gunshot, and Kate fell. *No! Please, no!*

Lila dropped to the ground, covering her head with her hands as multiple shots rang out; she heard the whizzing of the bullets as they flew over her head. And then they stopped. Hesitantly, she opened her eyes, moved her gaze upwards, focusing on the crumpled figure twenty feet or so in front of her.

*Kate!* Lila craned her head around to take in the scene behind her, where the first shot had come from. Grey smoke curled up from under the hood of the SUV; bullet holes riddled the silver metal. And there, by the twisted metal, lay Wes, blood pooling beneath him, the gun still clutched in his cooling fingers.

Lila had to get to Kate. It was the only thought in her mind after she clocked Wes' inert form. Pushing through her panic, she struggled to her knees, cradling the unborn life within her, willing the child to be alright.

"Stay on the ground!" a voice shouted at her.

For one awful moment, everything was silent. Then she heard a groan. It was Kate. Lila watched helplessly as she writhed in pain; she didn't know if Kate was conscious or not, if she was going to live or die. She knew only that she had to reach her.

"Kate!" she screamed and was in the smallest way, relieved to see police rushing to Kate's side, a female officer kneeling beside her. A pair of black boots filled her vision, then a hand, reaching, offering her assistance.

"Can you stand? Are you injured?" voices were asking Lila. More sirens were coming now, an ambulance. She turned her gaze upwards, connecting with the officer's, grasping at his hand, hauling herself up.

She pushed at him as soon as she was on her feet, but he held her tight as paramedics rushed to Kate. "Let them do what they can," the man's voice said calmly, but there was no way that she was going to not be by Kate's side, not hold her hand, not look into those eyes, if these were to be her last moments on earth. She forced her way from the halfhearted grip and limped towards her love.

Kate's eyes were fluttering as Lila approached. Flecks of blood covered her face, her hair. Her hands kept trying to push at the paramedics. "I'm fine. I'm fine," she kept saying over and over, even as the blood oozed from the hole in her side. The paramedics had cut the t-shirt away from the wound and randomly, Lila realized it was Kate's favorite, The Rolling Stones one, and all she could think in the moment was how upset Kate would be when they found out they'd ruined her favorite t-shirt.

# 32

It wasn't the first time Lila had seen those green eyes looking up at her since the shooting, but it was the first time since that day that they held any sort of recognition in them; Kate was finally truly waking. The doctors and nurses would want to know, to check her out for any permanent damage, though they didn't expect any. It had been two days since the decision was made to wake her from her coma.

Her eyes fluttered open. "Lila," she said, trying to bring her eyes into focus on the blurry face before her.

"I'm here, love, you're ok," Lila responded, taking Kate's hand in hers.

"So, I'm not dead, that's good."

"You scared the hell out of me, you know."

"I got a pretty good scare myself," she croaked, her throat still raw from being intubated. "Is Wes dead?"

"Yeah, we don't have to worry about him anymore. We'll be alright." Lila didn't know when or even if she was going to tell her the truth about Cecile. After everything else they'd been through, though, she knew it was best to get the truth out there.

"Are you ok? Is everything ok with the baby?" Kate quickly interjected, the fog of anesthesia slowly fading, giving rise once more to panic.

"We're both fine, I promise," she squeezed her hand. "I don't know how, but everything is fine." Kate coughed, trying to clear her throat again. "Let me get you a water," Lila stood and Kate gasped.

"How long have I been out?" she whispered, taking in Lila's much more noticeably pregnant figure. Kate's eyes welled with tears as suddenly, she realized just how close she'd come to death, to leaving Lila and their child alone, or to being the one left alone herself. "I'm going to be sick," she managed.

Lila was instantly back at her side, "About a month, but everything is ok."

"A month? You're not telling me something! I can't walk or something!"

Lila raised a brow, a grin on her face as she watched her girlfriend thrash about on the hospital bed, legs and all. "You. Are. Fine."

Kate realized her body seemed in working order, that she was panicking for no reason, and calmed down. "Why was I out so long then?"

"It was a medically induced coma, so you could heal. Kate, we need to talk about Wes. I'm sure you don't want to, but I have to tell you something."

Tears streamed down Kate's pale cheeks as Lila told her about Wes' confession; that he had been the one to take Cecile's life. That he had always been the one to stand between her and happiness. Their hands clasped in thankfulness that Wes had not taken theirs; that come what may, they would have each other.

———

Kate stood staring at the blooming mountain landscape, hands thrust into the pockets of her jeans, her nose pressed to the glass of the floor to ceiling window of her home studio. If she turned, Lila's unfinished portrait would stare back at her, judging her. She hadn't been able to bring herself to touch it after the shooting.

She'd barely even been able to touch Lila; she'd taken to sleeping in a guest room, not wanting her endless tossing and turning to keep Lila awake. She couldn't sleep at all without pills, barely ate. She could feel what they had slipping away, knowing she had the power to stop it, but incapable of making a move.

The guilt she felt at putting Lila and their unborn child in danger was almost unbearable. She took a deep breath, letting the moisture from her lungs fog the glass. Occasionally, she felt a momentary stitch with her breath, a reminder of her healed wound. She closed her eyes and leaned her head against the cool glass, letting tears slide down her cheeks.

————

Lila stood outside the closed door, her hand hesitating, raised to knock. She was trying to be patient with Kate, letting her know it was ok to not be ok; what Wes had put them through was traumatic, but after Kate returned home from the hospital, she shut down and Lila was at a loss. Her pleas for Kate to seek professional help went unheeded; there were only so many nights she was willing to sleep next to an empty space where Kate should be.

Kate's head turned at the shuffling outside the studio door; *Lila*. Lila, who had almost died because of her. Lila, who tried to pretend like life was going to be normal again. Lila, who she loved more than anything else in this world. Lila, and their daughter, who she was failing. She turned and threw open the door, shocking Lila, who jumped back as quickly as her seven months pregnant body would allow.

"I'm going for a ride," she barked, pushing past her stunned girlfriend. Lila knew Kate kept a vintage motorcycle in the garage, but she'd promised Lila the first time she had noticed it, that her riding days were done; what she had was too important. Now, after everything, that's where Kate was heading. It felt like a betrayal.

"Kate!" Lila started after her, up the stairs to the six-car garage that housed a variety of Kate's toys.

Kate had grabbed her leather jacket on the way out, her helmet sat between her hands as she straddled the machine. "Kate! You promised you wouldn't do this!"

Kate squashed the helmet over her curls, turned the ignition key, opened the throttle, and revved the engine before leaving Lila standing in an empty garage.

―――――

She had always been a careful rider in that she respected the machine and road; she wasn't riding like that now. Kate took every curve as low and fast as she could until she hit the main highway. The anger she felt towards herself, towards Wes, the inability she felt to connect with the woman she loved; it all welled up inside her until she screamed. She screamed into the cool night air, pushing the bike to its top speed. The old Royal Enfield rumbled beneath her and suddenly, as her screaming died, she could breathe.

Three hours later, Lila heard the bike returning up the long driveway. When Kate opened the door of the house, she was ready. "Don't ever fucking do that to me again!" Lila said. There were angry tears in her eyes as she spoke, her voice low and serious. "I know you've got some romantic, fatalistic, English thing about death, but I don't. I watched you get shot. I thought you were dead. The love of my life, gone. But you lived, Kate. You're alive, you're here with me, with us!"

Kate stood silently, head bowed, unsure if she could meet Lila's eyes. "I won't," her words barely above a whisper, "I'm not going anywhere."

"You need help, Kate," Lila said, "more than I can give."

"I know. I'll do whatever I need to. I swear."

Lila approached as she would a skittish dog; Kate hadn't let her hold her since the shooting. She reached for Kate's hand, which jerked involuntarily back, but Lila held tight, placing it against her belly. Kate had never felt the baby kick. Now Lila would not take no for an answer.

Lila could see it in her eyes, the shift, the spark come back into them as the tiny flutter within her responded to Kate's touch.

"This is our daughter." Lila's other hand held Kate's chin, forcing Kate's eyes to meet hers for what felt like the first time in weeks. "You told me you would be here for me; for her. You aren't alone anymore. We are a family."

Kate's lips crashed against hers. "I swear to you," Kate mumbled through the kiss and tears, "I swear I won't fuck up again."

Lila pulled away. "Of course you'll fuck up again, and so will I," her mood had lightened, the streaks of tears drying on her cheeks, "being a mess sometimes and fucking up is part of it. But, we'll get through this, and everything else that comes along together."

"I love you," Kate laughed through her own drying tears.

"Damn straight you do! Now come here and kiss me."

———

Lila woke the next morning to the tantalizing as ever smell of coffee and, oddly enough, bacon; it was odd because there was never any food in the morning unless she made it. Kate giggled as Lila entered the kitchen. "What?" Lila grumbled.

"I think you've reached the waddling stage, dear," she said, beaming.

Lila ran a hand over her belly. She certainly felt like she'd expanded to massive proportions overnight. "If I wasn't so tired, I might throw something at you for that."

Kate smirked and stood, squeezing Lila's shoulders and kissing her on the cheek. "It's a very graceful waddle, love."

"I was going for adorable," Lila grinned.

"That too," Kate said. "You sit down, I've attempted breakfast."

Lila quirked a brow, but did as she was told; Kate would hear no complaints from her girlfriend about being off her feet and waited on by a beautiful woman.

"So," Kate called from the kitchen; Lila had weeks ago abandoned any attempt at heaving herself onto the high stools around the island. She was currently seated in the small breakfast nook. "I may have stayed up all night after you fell asleep."

"Making breakfast?"

Kate sauntered back in, a plate piled high with bacon and a decaf coffee for Lila. "Painting," she said, placing the plate and mug on the table.

"Kate!" She noted now the streaks of paint on Kate's silk pajama top, in her hair.

Her lips drew back in a bright, wide smile. "Go look in the studio."

"Your studio?" Lila couldn't believe it, Kate hadn't once let her in that sacred space.

Lila trudged heavily down the stairs, and for the first time, could see past the thick wooden door. Tears rolled down her face as she saw her portrait for the first time; the piece Kate could not finish before the shooting and wouldn't touch after. She felt Kate's arms wrap gently around her, felt her lips pressed to her neck, felt her hair tickle an earlobe. Lila turned in the embrace. "Just like that?"

Kate knew she didn't just mean finishing the painting. "No," she said, "but it's a start, and we'll get through it together, as a family," her words echoing Lila's from the night before.

**One Month Later...**

The scar was barely visible anymore, just a circular indentation in her side. Still, her fingers ghosted over the tiny beads of her gown, over the healed wound. Kate thought of what she'd almost lost that day, including her own life. She'd come through it though, all three of them had. Meeting Lila at that party eight months ago changed so much in her life, and all of it for the better.

It was the opening night of her show, the biggest one of her life, but she knew now that it wasn't the show that was going to make it so special. She closed her eyes, taking a breath, feeling the soft velvet of the small box in her hand.

"Kate?" Lila called down the hallway. "Kelli is blowing up my phone, wondering where we are!"

"I'm here, love!" she said, rounding the corner and taking Lila's breath away.

Kate dropped to her knee, the light sparking off the sapphire beading of her gown as it pooled around her.

"Kate?" Lila almost tripped over her. "Are you alright?"

"I know this is ridiculously old-fashioned," she started, and Lila froze as she watched Kate produce the small velvet box. "Would you do me the honor of being my wife?" she said.

Lila couldn't speak, she just kept staring down at the ring, the emerald glittering in the chandelier's light.

"Kate," she breathed finally, not believing that only eight months ago she'd been single, just starting a new job, and now, she was about to be a mother, moving across the country and this glorious creature was down on her knee, asking her to be her wife.

Lila realized her mouth was hanging open and made a concerted effort to close it. She shook her head, feeling the tears come; she had not been expecting this. "Yes!" she saw the tension in Kate's body relax and she reached for Kate's hand to help her up. The two women stood, broad smiles on their faces, tears pricking at their eyes.

"Damn it!" Kate said, laughter in her voice. "Jenna is going to kill us for ruining our makeup!"

"Do you mind?"

"Not in the least, my love." Kate kissed her deeply, both melting into the other, standing still for one moment.

None of the past seemed real to her, Kate realized, as she stretched her hand toward Lila, her new ring glittering. She was beaming up at Kate from the seat of the limo at the entrance to the museum. Kate's name was written in large black letters on banners flanking the entrance, and as the two women stood together, flashes exploded around them.

———

Kate stood at the podium, as beautiful a sight as Lila had ever seen. She sat at a small table placed to the side of the audience just for her, standing for any amount of time no longer an option in her heavily pregnant state.

"As you may know," Kate began, "its been something of a year for me," there was laughter mingled with solemn nods from the crowd, "I would just like to acknowledge the person who has inspired me, who has re-ignited my love for my craft, and who has this very evening done me the great honor of becoming my fiancée," her face broke into a wide grin as the crowd released an audible gasp, "Ms. Lila Croft." Her eyes met Lila's, and she winked, blowing her a kiss.

# Epilogue

Screams of joy followed the little girl down the snow covered slope; her mothers following close behind as she made wide slow 's' down the mountain. The family was a familiar sight on the mountain over the last few years. Every once in a while a tourist would recognize the famous duo and stop to watch as they attempted to teach their daughter to ski, but they'd lived there long enough that the locals considered them among their own.

Kate laughed loudly as she found herself on her backside, her three-year-old daughter tangled up in her legs and skis. Tears of amusement pricked at Lila's eyes as she stopped next to the two and pulled her daughter free, giving her wife a wide smile. "You two alive?"

Kate sat up, dusted the snow from her pants, and returned her wife's beaming smile. "Think so," she ruffled the little girl's blonde curls before hauling herself up, "though I think Stella's got it out for her mom, don't you?" The little girl broke into a naughty grin before grumbling that she was ready for hot chocolate and chicken nuggets.

"Well then, lunch time it is!" Lila bent down and helped her daughter click out of her skis, putting them over her shoulder with her own as Kate scooped the girl into her arms.

"I'm so proud of you," her nose nuzzled the girl's. She readjusted her daughter on a hip and pulled Lila close. "You too love." As they made their way into the lodge, there were nods of greeting from other locals and a broad grin from Jenna as she spotted the three.

She waved and bent down, folding Stella in her arms. "Have you missed me?" She asked the little girl, who feigned disinterest.

"No," Stella said, and Jenna's fiancé let out a snort of laughter behind her.

"Oh, hush," she shot a look at Lasse, the sweet, dashing ski bum/contractor she'd met and promptly fallen for last season. She put the girl down and pulled a bundle from her bag. "Hand this to your moms."

Kate clapped her hands together while Lila looked bashful. "Oh, you got it! Let us see!" Stella reluctantly handed over the pile of papers. Lila and Kate had been expecting it. It was an advanced copy of their cover of The Times. "The New Old School," it read across the top and there, splashed across the page, was a large photo of Lila and Kate in their joint studio. For the last two years they'd worked on bringing back the craft of art, and they'd succeeded. Their last show sold out before the opening, and they were being hailed for the rise of a new classical movement.

"What do you think?" Jenna asked.

"I think we look happy." Kate smiled.

"That's because we are," Lila said, kissing her wife as their daughter hugged her mothers' legs.

**The End**

# Also by Riley West

Pirate's Queen

**An abducted ruler. A brave buccaneer. Will these two women sail into a sensuously tempting alliance?**

Queen Lucia of Moranth secretly yearns for adventure. Focused on the seriousness and monotony of regal responsibilities, the intelligent royal prepares for war when she learns a cruel cousin seeks her hand in marriage. But her plans are derailed when she's kidnapped and stolen away on a ship belonging to a striking lady.

Alessandra D'Allyon despises the monarchy that killed her mother. Yet the new pirate captain is less than pleased to discover her crew holding the sovereign hostage without her permission. And she can barely resist her saucy guest's advances when the alluring woman attempts a seduction.

Failing to convince the quippy commander into a roll between the sheets, Lucia lands in the midst of a battle after a rival vessel attacks. But when Alessandra ends up marooned with her gorgeous captive, working together to survive on a remote island stokes desires that can no longer be denied.

Will this unlikely pairing's complicated passions forge a bond that lasts forever?

*Pirate's Queen* is the spicy first book in the Shades Of The Seas lesbian romance series.

Printed in Great Britain
by Amazon

21836225R00148